W

# DEAD MAN'S RANGE

# DEAD MAN'S RANGE

Lauran Paine

Chivers Press • G.K. Hall & Co.
Bath, England    Waterville, Maine USA

This Large Print edition is published by Chivers Press, England, and by G.K. Hall & Co., USA.

Published in 2001 in the U.K. by arrangement with Golden West Literary Agency.

Published in 2001 in the U.S. by arrangement with Golden West Literary Agency.

U.K. Hardcover    ISBN 0-7540-4595-1    (Chivers Large Print)
U.K. Softcover    ISBN 0-7540-4596-X    (Camden Large Print)
U.S. Softcover    ISBN 0-7838-9565-8    (Nightingale Series Edition)

The text of this Large Print edition is unabridged.
Other aspects of the book may vary from the original edition.

Set in 16 pt. New Times Roman.

Printed in Great Britain on acid-free paper.

**British Library Cataloguing in Publication Data available**

**Library of Congress Control Number: 01-131936**
**ISBN 0-7838-9565-8 (lg. print : sc : alk. paper)**

C405177913

# CHAPTER ONE

'As simple as falling off a log,' Coleman said to Hugh Benedict. 'Old Fortier owned the land and held it against all comers red white an' brown to the day of his death. That's about the size of it, Hugh. If she won't sell voluntarily, there's no way you can make her do it. Besides that, she's not an ordinary female; you go pushing for trouble and you'll think the sky fell on you.'

Benedict stood by the window gazing out upon the bustle and bedlam of tent-town Denver with his back to U.S. Marshal Jack Coleman. He was one inch over six feet tall, lean, dark, and smiled easily, sometimes because he was amused, sometimes because smiling hid his true feelings. He was a good man with a gun as successful gamblers often had to be, and he was a resourceful man.

He turned and considered grizzled Coleman's faded, tough blue eyes, and he smiled showing even big white teeth which starkly contrasted with his nut-brown rangeman's colouring.

'It's interesting how people want time to stand still,' he said. 'What old Jules fought for and won fifty, sixty years ago, isn't the same land at all, Jack. It isn't even frontier any longer in the sense old Jules knew it.

Colorado's a federal territory now. There are roads and army posts and even things like the telegraph; things old Jules never dreamed possible.' Benedict strolled over and halted before Coleman's desk. 'Why does this slip of a girl believe it's all the same as it was when her father was alive?'

Coleman reached up to scratch his chin lightly and put a sardonic gaze upwards and outwards at handsome Hugh Benedict, and he dryly said, 'Well now, son, if we knew what makes folks as they are, why I reckon we'd know how to head off some of the unlikely things they do. But that doesn't change anything where Meredith Fortier is concerned, and you take it from your pappy's old wartime pardner, Hugh. She owns the land legal-like, fair-and-square. If she says she doesn't want your beef in her valley—that's it.'

'The law'll back her up. Is that it, Jack?'

'To the limit, Hugh, so don't go an' do anythin' that'll put you'n me on opposite sides of the fence.'

'Jack; that Fortier Valley is sixty miles long and—'

'I know how big Fortier Valley is, Hugh. I first rode the length and width of it before your paw even met your maw, an' the size doesn't change a thing. It's hers, boy. If she says for Hugh Benedict to keep out—you keep out.'

Benedict rocked up onto his boot-toes and

2

rocked down again. He looked long and thoughtfully at U.S. Marshal Jack Coleman and he blew out a big breath. 'Funny, isn't it,' he murmured. 'When I was a gambler men liked me and women hated me. I got my stake, quit cards and dice, and still women don't like me.'

Coleman had no comment along those lines so he said, with an air of finality, 'Colorado is a big territory, son. You don't need part of Fortier Valley anyway. Go on up north with your grazin' outfit; there's all kind of fine free land up there just beggin' to be taken up an' claimed.'

'Yeah,' said bronzed, lean and smiling Hugh Benedict. 'Well, Jack, it's been nice talking to you. We'll probably meet again.'

The marshal got up, stepped around his desk and opened the office door. 'Let me hear from you,' he said. 'It's a strange thing how much you resemble your paw when he was your age. Sort of jolted me when first I laid eyes on you.' As Benedict passed on out of the office Coleman looked after him and said: 'I hope you're not like your paw in some ways though, boy. Goodbye.'

Benedict turned and threw a smile over his shoulder, passed on out into the dusty springtime street, crossed through a stream of pedestrians to the big black horse at the yonder rack, stepped over leather and reined northward out of town.

3

There was a constant tangle of traffic all the way to the northward Fort Collins road. There was a big strike up north and miners of every kind and description clogged the roads with their outfits, sometimes good stout wagons, sometimes push-carts with two toiling, usually bearded, men drawing them along. There were dozens of horsemen and also dozens of hired four-seated high-wheeled wagons pulled by four or six stout mules. Everything that went with the wildly unpredictable saga of a big, new gold strike was there making tracks northward out of Denver. It was colourful; it was also dusty and there was no direction at all to the streaming-past mass of anxious humanity, therefore one frequently saw battles-royal at roadside where travellers had locked wheels or bumped rigs, and got into a fight.

Benedict, being astride instead of atop four wheels, could avoid most of that hurrying tangle of humanity simply by taking to the slopes or the plains parallel to the Fort Collins road, also heading northward. But six miles out he turned westward through an empty pass where black-hulking mountains rose to blot out a large square of azure sky, and after that he was almost entirely alone.

A few of that sweating horde showed up now and then along the rims seeking short-cuts to the goldfields, but not many and even those few did not come down into the enormous

4

basin where red-backed cattle with great-curving wicked horns, showed across that greeny expanse of lush land.

There was a canvas-topped wagon near the bisecting creek out there, and experienced hands had stretched a texas—a big flap of square canvas—out from the wagon's south side to form a shady spot near a rope-corral where mounds of tangled saddlery and other camp-gear lay strewn.

This was a typical cow-camp where men lived while on the move. There was a stone-ring to confine the cooking-fire and a black old dented coffee pot of large proportions always simmered there; men coming in or heading out made almost a ritual of tanking up on black java before going on past.

Benedict rode straight for that wagon-camp, his low-crowned, stiff-brimmed California black hat tipped down to shield his eyes. Several men rose up where they'd been squatting cross-legged beneath the texas and watched him approach. They were tough-looking, unkempt men. They looked half wild and as rough as a pine-knot. There were four of them, but as that four stood slouched awaiting Benedict's arrival, an older, squattier man with legs so badly saddle-bowed he resembled a wishbone, came scooting from inside the wagon and joined those other four. But this man wore no gun and he had a flour-sack apron tied around his middle. He was the

5

*cosinero*—the cow-camp cook. Among drovers this man's position was somewhat difficult to pin down; he was more often than not the doctor, the veterinarian, the arbiter of disputes, the preacher who read over some lonely grave from the Good Book, and he was also ordinarily as cantankerous, overbearing and troublesome as old crippled-up cowboys usually got to be.

It was this bandy-legged gnome of a man who walked away from the others, poured a cup of coffee and stood by with it as Benedict came up, swung down, and dropped his reins, hitched his black Prince Albert coat up so that it hung clear of his ivory-butted .45, and wordlessly squatted beside the fire ring to accept and sip that tin cup of black death.

'Well,' he said, as the four riders and the *cosinero* came wordlessly up and stood there waiting, 'it was a pure waste of time. Coleman said no. Said Fortier Valley's legally hers, and as well as said if we tried goin' on in, he'd be on our tails.'

The cook let loose with a lengthy if not particularly colourful string of curses, shook his head angrily and jabbed a stubby thumb at the northward mountains. 'What can we do,' he demanded. 'Go out'n try drivin' three thousand wild Idaho cattle alongside all them silly goldminers an' other riff-raff on the Fort Collins trace, or rub liniment on the critters to make 'em sprout wings and fly over these

6

blasted, consarned mountains?'

Benedict finished his coffee, flung away the gritty dregs, tossed aside the tin cup and raised up to stand with both thumbs hooked in his shell-belt. 'Why no, Stumpy,' he said to the *cosinero,* gently smiling. 'We go through Fortier Valley.'

Those four rangeriders gravely nodded at this pronouncement. There was nothing in their faces to indicate they'd ever thought Hugh Benedict would do anything else. One of them, a red-necked, hard-eyed, tousle-headed big man named Cowan—Art Cowan—said, 'She sure won't object to us just trailin' through, for gosh sakes. It's not like we're still tryin' to claim a piece of her valley.'

Benedict shrugged and smiled mirthlessly over at Cowan. 'There's just one thing about women I can swear to, Art. Their unpredictability, their unreasonableness, their damned, completely illogical approach to everything.'

Cowan listened and looked dubious about those impressive words and said, 'Well; does all that mean she will or she won't let us take the cattle through?'

'It means,' said Hugh, 'that I plain don't know what she'll let us do.'

'In that case,' drawled a lean, quiet man with deep-set grey eyes and a slash of a mouth, whose name was Tex Rathbone, 'I'd say let's just point 'em at her valley and cross anyway.'

7

'We may have to do that,' said Hugh. 'But first, just to keep things straight, we'll make an effort to reason with her.'

'Humph!' growled Stumpy. 'It didn't work before an' it won't work now. That there female-woman just plain don't like men. Specially if they got three thousand cattle along with 'em.'

Benedict said to Art Cowan, 'Rig me out a fresh animal and I'll ride over there again.'

'You'll need company,' said Cowan, making no immediate move to depart.

Benedict shook his head. 'They'll let a lone rider through. What could her men fear from just one man? Naw; this time I'll try it by myself.'

Cowan started to turn away but before he walked on he grumbled, 'They just could bury you up there too. She's got a rough crew in her damned valley.'

Tex Rathbone leaned upon the wagon's big rear wheel nodding agreement with Cowan's departing remark and gazing stonily at Benedict. 'What we should've done,' he said, 'was drive through first, then try'n talk land with her.'

Hugh smiled over into Rathbone's flinty face. 'It's always better to have hindsight than foresight,' he said. 'The trouble is—folks aren't born with it, Tex, and who'd guess one girl would own all that land and have all that iron in her makeup?'

8

'They got womenfolk like that down in Texas, Hugh.'

'This is Colorado, Tex.'

'Well, I'll make a bet she's got a Texas pappy or mammy—or *some* Texas blood in her *somewhere*.'

Stumpy struck one palm with the fist of his other hand. 'That's right,' he pronounced to them all. 'To be this cantankerous she's got to have Texas blood in her. Now when I was at Eagle Pass back in—'

'Hey, Stumpy,' said a mild-looking young cowboy with laughing big blue eyes whose name was Milton Stillwell, 'don't start tellin' us about the lousy war again. We're about on the verge of a war all our own as it is.'

'You,' said Stumpy Caldwell fiercely, 'don't know your place. Young pumpkins your age are supposed to be seed and not heard.'

Benedict removed his black frock coat, stepped over and threw it inside the wagon. He fished out a leather rider's coat of knee-length with fringe down each arm and across the yoke-line which was stained and shiny from much rough use, shrugged into it and said, 'Feel better. There are some things about towns I never liked. Gettin' spruced up like a Christmas tree was one.' He turned and walked over where Cowan was shuffling forward leading a fresh horse. When those two came together the little smile down around Hugh Benedict's lips was genuine enough.

9

'I'll take a bedroll,' he said. 'No sense in killing good horseflesh just to get back here in time to risk poisoning from Stumpy's cooking. I'll bed down somewhere in the hills and meet you at the wagon sometime tomorrow.'

Cowan nodded, handed over the reins and cast a narrowed look on over where a notch showed in the onward hills. 'Good luck, Hugh,' he muttered. 'Keep an eye peeled for that black-bearded, black-hearted rangeboss of hers. He looked to me like a feller who'd shoot first and look second.'

'Yeah,' murmured Hugh, mounted, flung a careless wave at his men and booted the fresh horse over into a mile-eating lope heading north-westward towards the notched-out pass.

## CHAPTER TWO

An empire, like a chain, is no stronger than its weakest link and ordinarily vulnerability hinges upon simple economics. Take away the markets and the corroding begins. But as long as the markets remain strong, so does the empire.

That's how it had been with the Fortier outfit ever since Denver and the other little mushrooming mining towns in upper Colorado boomed, and old Jules Fortier, dead five years now, had ridden the crest of that economic wave to amass a fortune in land and cattle, and tough, hard resolve. Jules had come out of New England, out of that rock-ribbed and flinty world of iron-willed men and bitter-lipped women. He had first seen what was to become Colorado Territory as a young trapper and mountain man. He had laid claim to a huge valley, had brought in cattle and had started his empire. His wife had died there in Fortier Valley and so had his only son, victims of an Indian war. Where these losses might have broken another man, they only instilled in old Jules a more fierce determination to triumph, and he *had* triumphed too. He had hired the toughest riders he could find, but he hadn't only fought with guns and his native wiles to preserve his empire. He had hired eastern attorneys to push through his claim to Fortier Valley, and he'd won there too.

Then old Jules had turned up his toes leaving behind his empire and his only surviving heir, Meredith, a doe-eyed girl of seventeen, named Meredith after New England custom, Meredith being her mother's maiden name.

But he'd also left behind something else; his rock-hard crew of rangeriders under the foremanship of black-bearded, big and fierce old Ed Morrow. Jules had found Morrow in a tank-town jailhouse roaring like a bull, charged with beating a man to death with his fists, and Jules had liked what he'd seen because Ed Morrow was not an intelligent man, he was simply undeviatingly loyal, brave as a lion and as uncompromising as the devil himself. Ed Morrow had been exactly the kind of man old Jules had been seeking, so he'd bought him off, taken him to Fortier Valley, given him the job as Fortier's rangeboss, and in his declining years old Jules had at long last been able to sit back and smile. The same savage ferocity old Jules had ruled his empire with in former years, continued under the leadership of loyal, six-feet-two-inch, two-hundred-and-ten-pound, black-bearded and swarthy big Ed Morrow.

Five years later with old Jules mouldering under the good sod of his valley, with Meredith now twenty-two instead of seventeen, the ghost of Jules Fortier still rode the land.

No one entering Fortier Valley alone in search of work or food or a place to briefly rest before riding on, was ever turned back. Western tradition forbade that. But woe to the man or men who cast covetous eyes upon the great log buildings or the creeks, or the miles upon miles of rich emerald land.

And wealth had rolled in. Each time there was a gold strike somewhere, Denver nearly burst its seams with adventurers, miners, drovers, gamblers, even foreign immigrants in droves, all of whom had to eat. Fortier beef went out through the eastward pass to the Fort

Collins trace, turned southward and wound up in the abattoirs of a dozen large Denver meat processors, and the return trips were made with gold-laden saddlebags.

Fortier Valley, like Fortier Ranch, was strategically located. Others might grub for ore but Meredith Fortier simply ran her ranch and let the normal processes of progress bring her wealth and power, because old Jules had been a man of rare foresight.

She was a girl-turned-woman at twenty-two; she was poised and confident and thoroughly capable. There was a lot of old Jules' drive and ambition in her. There was also much of his cold logic and tough decisiveness. And yet Meredith was quite handsome. She was grey-eyed, black-haired, long-legged and high-breasted. She could turn a man to salt with her cruel stare, or she could melt all his reserves with a smile. She controlled her men through big Ed Morrow, who was, at fifty-five, young enough to tug at his great beard when she passed by, and old enough to view her as he might have viewed a daughter if he'd ever had one.

They didn't always agree; no strong man and strong woman always could agree, but over the years since Jules' death they had worked out a sequence which was satisfactory to both. Meredith would give the orders. If Ed thought they were good he carried them out to the letter. If he did not he would bluntly say

13

why not; he would offer alternatives. Sometimes she would accept, sometimes she would remain unmovable. It was a basically sound relationship; the only compromise possible between two iron-willed people. She respected big Ed, even when he showed his cruel side towards the outlaws and squatters who plagued Fortier Ranch from time to time, and he on the other hand also respected her, viewing her as he did as less of a beautiful woman and more of his personal responsibility, which was his nature, and which, at fifty-five, would be his nature until the day he died.

That's why he said, as he sat atop a rocky ridge watching that solitary black-hatted rider wind upwards from down below, 'You head on home. The boys an' I'll handle this,' and rolled his heavy brows downwards into a cruel scowl at that small figure down below. 'The wise ones take no for an answer. The unwise ones keep tryin'. This Benedict feller's got to learn his lessons the hard way.'

Meredith sat her saddle gravely considering that unsuspecting rider coming ahead through the pass which separated Fortier Valley from the outside world. 'Let him come on, Ed. I'm curious.'

Morrow tugged at his beard. There were three Fortier Ranch riders hunkering along the rims behind them also watching Benedict. They were bronzed, lean, capable men with

14

guns and lariats, with the directness to them which went with men formed and sustained by their raw, half-wild environment. Any one of them would rise up, dust off his breeches at a word from Ed or Meredith, ride down to meet Hugh Benedict, challenge him in fair-fight and kill him without a word or a speck of afterwards remorse. That's the only kind of men old Jules, and later on, Ed Morrow, ever hired to ride for Fortier Ranch.

Ed tugged at his beard and scowled blackly, but he did not immediately argue with Meredith. Instead, he said, 'Sometimes when they try to buy a piece of the valley an' we turn 'em away, they're wise enough to ride on, which is the way reasonable men should do. Sometimes not. This one, Meredith—this one is trouble. I never saw one of them smilin' ones with an ivory-stocked pistol who moved easy like Benedict does, that didn't have a yard of pure black iron up his back.'

'I'm just curious,' said the lovely girl, eyes still cast downward where that solitary horseman was winding uphill through the dusty springtime pass. 'He knows I won't sell to him. But he's got a big herd, Ed, and he's got to keep them clear of the Fort Collins road. I'm curious to hear what kind of an offer he'll make to get permission to drive them through Fortier Valley.'

'Well now that's not really the important thing,' stated Ed Morrow. 'The important thing, Meredith, is what he'll do when you tell him he can't drive through.' Morrow looked around where those three bronzed riders were squatting beside their horses quiet and watchful and tight-lipped. He faced forward, sighed and searched out that horse and rider again, kept his solemn black gaze upon both for a while longer, then said, 'Some day there'll be others making this same drive. As the Territory grows and fills up more'n more drovers'll be bringin' in beef. Eventually they'll take a piece of our market.'

Meredith shook her head. She had a degree of vision Ed Morrow lacked, which was part of old Jules' legacy to her. 'No matter how cheaply they buy their herds in Idaho or down south in California, Ed, by the time they've trailed them this far, paid all the tolls, the wages, absorbed all the losses and fatalities, they have to sell at the same high dollar we get just to make it worthwhile. And even then our profit is the greater one, so if some day the price drops we'll still be able to make money, and these adventurers won't. Then, they'll quit. They'll have to.'

Meredith looked at black Ed Morrow. He was struggling to comprehend this matter of economics, she knew. She also knew what he would do next because she'd grown up around him. When anything troubled Ed he shrugged his mighty shoulders in an annoyed manner like a bull in fly-time, and switched the subject.

16

Now, as Benedict hove up over the last switch-back and was within a mile of them, he lifted his shoulders, dropped them and growled, 'He's got four rugged-lookin' men working for him, and trouble could come from that direction.'

She smiled. 'He's a man who'd control his riders, Ed. He's like you were twenty years ago.'

'You were just a baby then, Meredith.'

'He's you all over again, Ed, only younger. As for that smile. It doesn't fool anyone. It didn't fool you and it doesn't fool me. Hugh Benedict is a determined man. As for letting him trail through Fortier Valley. Why not?'

Ed's head whipped around. His black gaze flashed. 'You wouldn't,' he said, making almost a command out of those two words. 'Meredith; his kind takes, they never give. He'd be back next year with another herd to trail on to the mining camps, and next year he wouldn't ask— he'd just drive on through.'

She had no wish to argue, certainly not in front of those three lean men listening back there where they finally began to straighten up beside their horses as the sound of oncoming steel horseshoes echoed on ahead, so she crossed both hands over the saddlehorn and waited out the emergence of Hugh Benedict around the last bend in the trail. Ed kept staring at her, seeing her not as she actually was but as he thought she should be.

17

But Benedict didn't see her that way at all when he swept around the final high lift and spotted the five of them awaiting him up there with their guns and their Fortier-branded horses. He saw her with rich sunlight shining across the ebony blackness of her hair. She was round-shaped and poised in his sight, heavy lips lying closed in gentle fullness, eyes the slatey colour of oaksmoke upon a wintry day full upon him, their expression shadowed and reserved towards him. Her breasts lightly lifted and lightly fell to her breathing. He rode that last hundred feet and drew rein without heeding black Ed Morrow or those three cold-eyed and careful men further back, refusing to allow a little wispy notion to come down from its secret place in his brain because it was the germ of an idea that he hadn't really had to make this ride so soon at all, but he'd wanted to. He had wanted to look once more at Meredith Fortier.

The pull of her presence had been that urgent since he'd ridden into Fortier Valley three days earlier to talk about buying land from her. Then, at her ranch, he'd argued and he'd cajoled, but she had so nearly thrown him off balance with her totally unexpected beauty he hadn't really been able to entirely concentrate on his arguments, so in the end she'd coolly turned him back. At least he felt that's what had happened; it was inconceivable to him that she could—a woman—out-think, out-argue, out-scheme him.

He touched his hatbrim to her in a casual yet gallant little gentlemanly gesture, and he said in his smiling way, 'I didn't expect such a reception, ma'am.' Then he dropped that hand and let it lie lightly along his right side where that ivory-stocked .45 was. 'I came alone, but you wouldn't have needed all these men anyway. I simply wanted to make you a proposition.'

Ed Morrow and the men behind him waited, their spirits hardened against Benedict, their bodies loose and easy but not entirely unprepared. They would listen and do nothing or they would draw and shoot to kill, it was one and the same to them.

Meredith sat over there waiting and saying nothing, her dead-level wintry gaze cool, indifferent. She was aware of Hugh Benedict but she was also sceptical of him and his handsome smile.

'I have three thousand head to move through to the camps. I can't take them up the Fort Collins trace—not with all those men and rigs using it. If I can trail through your valley and swing northward, I'm saved. If I can't . . .' Benedict lost his smile, gazed straight at her and shrugged. 'I'll be in trouble. If there was another way I wouldn't ask it. And if there was another way, Miss Fortier, you wouldn't have to grant it.'

'*Have* to grant it?' said Ed Morrow in his

bass voice, which was threateningly soft towards Benedict.

For the first time Benedict looked at the rangeboss. He was sombre to match Morrow's stiff defiance. 'This is my first trip through up here. I've been cutting my teeth on this trail ever since I left Idaho. Some places have been good to me, some have not. The ones that haven't I'll never pass over again. This is one of them, Morrow. I tried to be fair and buy a strip of land for my trail through. You and I both know I can't go any other direction, now that the Fort Collins road is impassable for wild cattle. If you were in my place, believe me, I'd never buck you.'

'That's something I'll never know for sure,' murmured Ed Morrow. Then his expression didn't soften any, but it turned cautious. Ed was evidently remembering Meredith's remark about perhaps letting the Idaho herd through Fortier Valley. He said, 'It's not up to me, Benedict.'

Hugh smiled, saying dryly, 'I think I'm probably lucky about that, Morrow.'

And Ed nodded. 'You are. I'd never in God's world let you through. Neither would Miss Meredith's paw.'

Benedict drifted his glance back to the girl and she met it as direct towards him as he was being towards her, but there was nothing to be read in her face beyond the faintest show of interest in him as he sat over there facing the

20

five of them cool and unafraid and waiting. She could obviously be as distant and detached when she wished to be as any man Benedict had ever known, and this troubled him. He wasn't used to women who thought and acted like men. It made him uncomfortable. He sat and watched her and waited.

'There is ample feed down where your herd is,' she coolly said to him. 'The water is good. That congestion out on the Fort Collins road will dwindle within a couple of weeks, Mister Benedict. Let your cattle rest and put on a little weight for that long, they need it.'

'Ma'am, the cattle can use the rest, sure, but this near the camps I need the money they'll bring.'

'The answer,' she said to him, 'is—no.' She started to turn away. 'Leave two men to watch this pass,' she said to Ed Morrow. 'Now let's get back.'


## CHAPTER THREE

The riders Ed Morrow detailed to remain at the pass were quiet men typical of their kind. If anything, they were as much like the Indians they'd helped wrench this uplands country away from as men could be. But this was a world which forged all its inhabitants, two-legged or four-legged, into the same hard mould. Survival mattered primarily. There were of course other considerations because the men like the animals had other drives, other reasons and motives, but always foremost was survival, so those two cowboys stood over there facing forward, watching Hugh Benedict, and neither of them turned even once to gaze after departing Meredith Fortier, big Ed Morrow, or that other rangerider. Their obligation was to protect not only the others but also themselves, so they stood watchful and ready until Benedict reached up, pushed back his hat, let off a long sigh and swung outwards and downward to stand over there beside his horse. He wasn't going to wrathfully explode, that much became gradually evident. He wasn't even going to call out to the departing riders with some final plea or some final threat. The two Fortier Valley men loosened up a little. One of them dug out his makings and went to work manufacturing himself a smoke. When he finished he held out the sack and papers towards Hugh Benedict.

He got a head-wag and a small, sardonic smile. 'Why?' he asked. 'I didn't even get the chance to offer her two-bits a head crossing fee. Why did she make up her mind so suddenly like that?'

The cowboy who wasn't smoking shrugged and opined that a woman is a woman and no man could say whatever made them say or do the things they said and did.

Benedict turned wry. There was a red sun dropping off towards some distant rims and the world was turning rusty from that reflected red light. 'How do I get the cattle to the camps now?' he asked.

That smoking cowboy considered the ragged tip of his cigarette and said, 'Mister, you got a real problem there. I've been in these hills six years now, an' I can tell you there just ain't but two ways: Up the trace or through Fortier Valley.'

'She leaves me no choice, boys.'

'Oh?' drawled the un-smoking cowboy. 'What d'you mean by that, mister?'

Benedict's tawny, gold-flecked brown eyes drifted to this man and lingered. 'Let me put it this way: If you were in my boots what would *you* do?'

The cowboy softly scowled as he ran this notion through his mind. In the end he gave the easiest answer by saying, 'I ain't in your place, so I don't have to come up with the answer to that.'

The other man looked out over the broken flow of southward country with a thoughtful expression and narrowed eyes. 'We been gatherin',' he said in a casual tone. 'We've been gettin' ready to do our springtime work—markin' and brandin'. Now, if she'd let you come through, mister, we'd be separatin' your critters from ours for a week of hard ridin', an' if I was to guess, I'd say that's what was in the back of her mind when she said you couldn't drift on through.'

But Benedict shook his head over this. 'No problem there,' he said. 'I've got four good men. We could push ours through and help you hold yours off, and afterwards we'd be glad to make up for the lost time by helping with the marking and branding.'

'Well,' said the smoking cowboy as he dropped his cigarette and ground it out underfoot, 'she said no—so no it is, mister.' He raised his candid eyes. 'Like Ed told you—it's her decision to make not his. And it sure ain't mine.'

Benedict stood a moment longer regarding those two before turning, stepping up over leather and gathering his reins. 'Good hunting,' he said and rode away, back down the trail the way he'd earlier arrived at this high-up, wind-blown place.

For as long as Benedict was in view those two Fortier riders remained at their point of vigil. The one who didn't smoke finally turned to his friend and said, 'You know what I think; I don't think that Benedict feller'll be so easy to turn back.'

The other man said, 'He's already turned back, Will. She said no and old Ed said no—and that's that. How long we supposed to stay up here anyway? This dang foolishness'll make us late for supper.'

'We'll make sure he heads for his camp;

24

that's about what Ed had in mind. But I still say Benedict's no quitter. 'You make a good study of him? He's not the turnin'-back kind. Nossir.'

'Well, what else can he do?'

'Push 'em up through this pass in the dark, for one thing. Try some such manoeuvre like that.'

'Aw hell, Will. He's not dumb enough to try an' force passage. We'd massacre him.'

The man called Will put a critical look over at his companion. 'Listen, bucko,' he said, 'I rode down to that wagon-camp with Ed day before yesterday to sort of scout 'em up down there. Ed wanted to see how their critters looked and what Benedict's crew was like.'

'I know. I saw you two head for the pass.'

'Yeah, maybe you did. But what you *don't* know is that this here Benedict's got a savvy outfit. Four men who look about as rough'n ready as they come.'

'All right,' assented the other cowboy. 'So he's got four an' we got five. If he had fifty he'd be a fool to try it through Fortier Valley. If we couldn't put 'em down Ed or Miz Meredith'd go fetch the law up here—and *then* where would this Benedict feller be?'

'I ain't particularly worried about where Benedict'd be, I'm worried about where *I'd* be.'

'Oh hell,' grumbled the other man, turning towards his animal, 'let's head for home. He won't try it, there won't be no trouble, an' I'm hungry as a bitch-wolf at whelpin' time.'

They got astride, turned their horses and started back down the north side of Fortier Pass. Below and on both sides further than either of them could see in the settling dusk, lay Fortier Valley, and coming upwards faint-soft and distant, was the lowing of cattle.

The blood-coloured sun lay hull-down against the far horizon, its final rays reddening all that intervening stretch of broken land, and somewhere out there between Fortier Valley and the far-away drop of land lay the Laramie Plains, the Laramie range of mountains, and all those mushrooming gold camps which were hungering for red beef. There was a mottled snake of a broad roadway winding up to those places choked with the teams and roadside smoking camps of men. Normally that road saw little enough traffic. Normally, when a drover got north of Denver with his Idaho beef his troubles would be over. But this was not a normal springtime and there lay the rub.

But a man who has breasted Idaho's wild Snake River in springtime and who has crossed the raw crags of a dozen sawtoothed mountain ranges, ploughed ahead through Indian hunting grounds and skirted all those little hungry settlements on the Colorado Road, and won out, wasn't likely to have come this far, to have victory in sight, then give up simply because a beautiful woman and a black-looking bearded rangeboss barred his way with their stubbornness and their unreasoning perversity.

Even if that man hadn't been by instinct a gambler, and by nature as unbending towards unreasonableness as Hugh Benedict was, he still wouldn't in all probability have given up this close to trail's end, because when a man gambled every dime he had in this world upon cashing in on a gold strike he had to be bold and resourceful and unflinching. If he allowed himself to be stalled or turned back he was ruined. If he could persevere another thirty days he could be rich for life. The sod of Colorado, like the sod of every other Western state or territory, held the bones of these prairie buccaneers who staked everything on such a risk, and for every one who had died struggling, there were ten more would survive the identical struggle. If men died in the crimson flame of gunfire, then they died, but to men like Hugh Benedict there were worse things than dying; being beaten, being a failure, was one of them.

So he didn't head back for his wagon-camp after that meeting up in Fortier Pass at all, and in fact he had never intended to return, not even when he'd smilingly told Art Cowan he might be gone all night. It wasn't in the nature of men like Hugh Benedict to give away all their plans, their dreams and their suspicions. They did what they thought had to be done.

Sometimes it wasn't ethical, sometimes it wasn't legal, but one thing it sure-Lord was—it was profitable.

He drifted back down that pass for a long shadowy couple of miles, until the switchbacks, the lifts and drop-aways had adequately concealed him from those two bored watchers up there, then he left the trail, angling around the fat haunch of a lower-down hill, kept to this trackless course until he was upon a windy little spiny ridge where he had a perfect, uninterrupted view of late-day Fortier Valley, then he struck out due northward in the direction of those solid old log buildings which were the headquarters of Fortier Ranch.

If you couldn't make a woman listen to you when she had four guns behind her, why then you went about it in some other way, but one thing you *didn't* do—you never gave up trying. Normally it would be simply a matter of masculine pride turned yeasty and prickly at being voted-down by a female. But now it was much more than that. It was a fortune in raw gold; it was independence for life. It was the *big gamble.* She'd got hers by inheritance, by being born to the right father at the right time. Well, Hugh Benedict's father had died young in a crowded saloon so all he'd inherited had been that ivory-butted .45—re-chambered from its original .41 calibre patch-and-prime kind of a weapon. Four years in the Confederate army had taught the elder

Benedict just one sure fact about life. A gun was formed to fit a bold man's grip. He'd bequeathed his lanky son that knowledge, plus something which Marshal Coleman knew but which Hugh only suspected—a certain calculating bold toughness that frequently spelled trouble.

He sat a long moment atop that flinty ridge looking down into the Fortier empire. A woman shouldn't own all this, he gravely told himself. Not by herself she shouldn't. Especially not a woman with the powerful hungers he suspected lay deep down in Meredith Fortier. A man should rule here. Not a black-bearded old bulldog of a fighting man with the narrowness that went with lifelong reliance upon guns and guts, but a man who would make Fortier Valley impregnable and richer than its founder's wildest dreams had ever envisaged.

Fortier Valley should belong to Hugh Benedict. So should the ruler of Fortier Valley belong to him. He shook out his reins to make the horse begin that long, shadowy descent. But first there were those three thousand Idaho cattle. First they had to cut up through this insular world to prove to a beautiful lady her law wasn't the only law. Afterwards— well—afterwards a man's steel will would prevail over a woman's steel will because that's the way life was, and that also was the way life should be. As an old Texan had once told him:

'Every feller'd like to be liked. Ain't a livin' man as wouldn't feel good inside to have folks smile when he rides past, my boy. But just you remember one thing: the nice fellers always finish last and the tough fellers wind up rich, so you make up your mind, Hugh, whether you want to be buried in a lousy pine box an' have a hundred blubberin' mourners standin' above you, or whether you want to go into the damned ground with a solid silver casket wrapped around you, because you can't be both rich and popular—and in the end just one thing's damned certain—you're going to die some day.'

He came down into the valley finally with a big old yellow moon hanging above the rampart-peaks as though it belonged here in Fortier Valley too, paving the empty night with its rich bright glow.

He was able to see little bunches of greasy-fat Fortier cattle here and there, able to hear that grunting sound as they heaved upright at sight of a horseman passing along.

He also saw several flashing-past bands of startled horses, steeldusts mostly. The kind of horses every lifelong saddleback-man stopped no matter where he was to admire them.

He also saw the rushing creeks fed from year-round overhead snowfields, that made Fortier Valley the fecund place that it was, and he speculated on old Jules, thinking that whatever else he might have been, old Fortier

30

had been a sagacious man. Then he smiled to himself. No matter how wise and careful-planning a man might be, Nature didn't always concur, for where old Jules should have left behind five stalwart, hard-riding sons to govern this empire, Nature had tricked him, had left only a daughter.

He saw guttering orange squares of light on ahead where the bunkhouse and the main-house lay squatly massive and dark in the ghostly moonlight. He made out the big log barn, the corral-network, the outbuildings placed seemingly at random, but craftily put to form a sort of wagon-circle upon the valley floor by dead Jules Fortier, and his eyes glowed at this. Old Jules might have stoutly declared at a dozen treaty-fires that he loved and respected and trusted his red brothers, but nevertheless he circled-up his ranch buildings in the time-honoured posture of defence.

A wise man left behind all the little fashionings of his hands to give an observant stranger an insight into what kind of a man he had been. Jules Fortier had been tough but he'd also been shrewd. As Hugh reined off into a little jutting spit of pines to hide his horse he thought he'd have liked to have known old Jules Fortier; thought he and old Jules would have understood one another, could have chuckled a little together even as they craftily watched one another for the opportunity to prove mastery.

31

He walked out of the trees straight over towards the lighted main-house, still half-smiling, and at the same time he kept a corner of the building between himself and that squatty bunkhouse.

The big yard lay silvery and empty. Down in the barn a horse stamped. Over at the bunkhouse some triumphant poker player bawled in rude glee. Hugh stepped up onto the main-house veranda, found the door and rolled one big fist across it, then removed his hat.

## CHAPTER FOUR

When Meredith opened the door lampglow back-grounded her in Benedict's sight. She was no longer attired in her riding clothes but wore now a full-fashioned ankle-length dress that flared from the hips downward and was tight from there upwards to accentuate her magnetic physical pull. Her wealth of ebony hair was caught near the back of her head with a little perky yellow ribbon and her fresh-scrubbed face, aside from showing astonishment at sight of Hugh Benedict standing there hat in hand, softly smiling down into her eyes, was soft-shadowed and very handsome.

In a voice as easy as an April wind over a

silver thaw, he said, 'You didn't give me a chance to finish, Miss Meredith. I wanted to make you an offer of a passage-fee.'

Her light-lying hand upon the door-edge convulsed and after the shock atrophied her eyes blazed out at him. He glided one booted foot forward to block the door's slamming and continued to gently regard her. He wagged his head at her.

'No need to get hostile,' he murmured. 'My intentions are the best.'

'The worst,' she rapped out at him. 'Do you realise that one call from me would get you killed?'

'But you wouldn't,' he said. 'You're a real lady, Miss Meredith. More than that—you're downright beautiful. Maybe you're queen of Fortier Valley, but you're sure a lot more than that too.'

'I should've left you to Ed,' she stated, but her voice sounded less flat towards him, less hostile. 'He knows how to handle your kind, Mister Benedict.'

'No'm, I don't believe he does. You see, Ed Morrow's a violent man, and violent men are fools.' He looked past into the warm-lighted and expensively furnished large parlour.

'If Ed's a fool, Mister Benedict, then what I need at Fortier Ranch is more fools, because he's kept men like you out.'

'Not like me, Meredith, because Ed Morrow's never tangled with a man like me before.'

'Oh?' she said coolly, watching his shadowed face, the flash of his white teeth against the bronzed colouring of his skin. 'You are something special?'

'Not special, just willing.'

'What does that mean, Mister Benedict?'

He removed that intruding foot, stepped back and rolled his head sideways. 'Call him, Meredith, and I'll allow him first shot.'

'You fool,' she tartly said, 'he'd kill you. And if he didn't there are four more of my men down there who would.'

'Not one at a time, ma'am.'

She tapped briefly with one small foot. She put her head gently to one side and ran a long look up and down him. She stepped aside and said, 'Come in, Mister Benedict.'

He stepped through, closed the door and glanced at this very masculine, very large and well-furnished big room with strong approval. 'You know,' he mused aloud, 'on the ride in here I told myself I'd have liked to have known your father.' He brought his bold, tawny gaze back to her face.

She turned and paced over where a gigantic stone fireplace black from many winters backgrounded her, making her seem almost fragile and definitely female. She swung around and watched him, and she told herself truthfully that her father *would* have liked this man. Her father had also been shrewd and relentless and able to smile, to show charm on the outside while on the inside he'd made his black plans.

'Finish what you came here to say, Mister Benedict. I'll listen. Then ride back where you came from.'

He put his low-crowned hat upon a little marble-top table, straightened up to his full height and swept a hand backwards in the unconscious gesture of a man accustomed to brushing a reassuring hand across that ivory-stocked gun on his hip. Lord but she was a picture over there aloof and cold towards him, high-breasted and round-shaped with her smouldering gaze and her heavy-lipped dark red mouth. He sighed. Perhaps it was simply that a lone man's thoughts turned magnetically towards the first really handsome woman he saw after being so long on the trail.

'Two-bits a head to cross your land,' he said. 'Payable in advance.'

'No.'

'Don't break me, Meredith, I'm a gambler. I've saved a long time to take my big plunge. I put together this herd with sweat and sleepless nights. I'm not saying this to elicit any sympathy, only to make you see that I didn't have the same opportunities you were born to, but I want the same things. I need to be an independent man with money and land and livestock.' His voice softened and roughened towards her at the same time. 'I need more,

35

but I can't have the rest of it by coming along hat-in-hand.'

'The answer is still no, Mister Benedict.'

He checked his words, stood gazing over at her. Finally he said, 'Why? I asked your two men that up at the pass. One of them said because you'd been gathering to brand and mark. Meredith, I have four top-hands. We'll keep the herds apart and after we're through your valley we'll come back and help you so there'll be no loss to you by our going through.'

'My rider,' she said dryly, 'was only partly right. It's true we've started gathering. It's also true we were doubtful about being able to keep six thousand head of cattle separated. But the main reason I refused up in the pass and still refuse here in my parlour, Mister Benedict—is because of you.'

He stood silent waiting for her to explain that but she didn't. She simply stood over there looking damnably desirable, watching his face which was now quite unsmiling, and her steady, wintry gaze towards him was as hard as iron. This, he told himself, was a look she'd inherited from her old pappy; this was the uncomprising stare of a person dedicated to resistance, and whatever *real* reason lay behind that resistance didn't so much matter because whether she would even admit what it was to herself or not, she was ready to give Ed Morrow and those other tough men her nod,

36

and that could definitely threaten his survival. And survival mattered.

It was a little like being challenged to lift a five hundred pound stone in some cow-town saloon for the drinks. First you mentally weighed the stone, next you tried to imagine just which way the thing might be gripped, and finally you wondered whether a sore back and strained ligaments for thirty days afterwards were worth the effort.

They were.

To many men they were not but to bold gambling men they were because a challenge heightened a man's self-pride, and triumph boosted it even more. But here and now, if he turned away and let her win for the second straight time in her ranch yard, the next time they met there would be contempt in those smoke-grey eyes. The next time she would triumph over him again, and every time after that they met he would sink still lower in her opinion until, finally, he would be quite unable to ever climb back, which would utterly destroy the final part of his plan, which was simply to possess this beautiful, strong-willed woman and everything that went with her.

'Is that answer enough for you?' she asked.

'No,' he candidly said. 'But you won't give a better one.'

'You don't need a better one, Mister Benedict. All you need is my decision, which is still no.'

'Spoken like a true queen of all she surveys,' he said softly, and reached out for his hat. 'I've heard it said many times that it takes two to make trouble, but I never agreed with that. It takes only one.'

She moved away from the fireplace, over by an oval lamp, and she gently wagged her head at him. 'Don't try it, Mister Benedict, because you couldn't possibly win.'

He lay a long, thoughtful glance upon her. 'Just tell me this much,' he said. 'If it's a personal dislike, is it because you don't want me to win my big gamble; you resent the thought of a stranger to your country cashing in on this mining boom?'

'Not at all,' she told him in her quiet, hard tone of voice. 'I know your kind. They are ruthless and calculating and dishonest, and if there's one thing Colorado *doesn't* need right now it's more men of that stripe.'

He considered arguing; considered saying that her father had also been bold and ruthless, and perhaps even dishonest; that all the strong men of this world were like that, or they remained anonymous members of the tiresome human herd. He even thought of relating to her what the rich old Texas cowman had told him years back. But he didn't. He lifted his hat, dropped it upon the back of his head and stepped silently over to the door. There, he turned with his left hand on the latch and said, 'Meredith, the Lord gives

38

beauty but I've noticed in my lifetime that he rarely gives beautiful women or handsome men what should go with beauty—good common sense. You're forcing me to fight you, and I'll tell you now because I may never have the opportunity to tell you this again, that I never in my life dodged a fight, and I never in my damned life saw anyone I wanted less to fight.'

He lifted the latch but didn't open the door because she spoke over to him in that same less hostile tone she'd used before when he'd candidly admired her.

'Don't fight me, Mister Benedict. In the first place you'd lose. Not just against Ed Morrow and my crew, but also against Jack Coleman who is U.S. Marshal down in Denver.'

'I know Coleman,' he murmured. 'My father before me knew him.'

She ignored that and said, 'You were told this afternoon to let your cattle rest where they are. There's plenty of rich feed and clean water. Within thirty days the Fort Collins road will be clear, then you can take them on up to the diggings. They'll be fatter. They'll bring you more money. I think I'm helping you with this advice.'

'Do you?' he softly said, looking straight into her eyes. 'Don't try to do me any favours because you don't know what you're talking about. There happens to be two more herds out of Idaho behind me. I've pushed like a dog to hold my lead and they've pushed hard to catch up because the first man to reach the diggings makes his killing and the others take second best. I can't wait thirty days, Meredith. Even if I wanted to, I couldn't.'

Her grace, her compelling beauty, even her open hostility which seemed to run hot and cold towards him, held him a moment longer over by the door. She was something a starved man could look upon and carry in his mind to the end of his days remembering every detail, every outline, every shadow as it now was, and none of that would ever dim out or alter even over the long, long years.

He opened the door and shook his head at her. 'I don't know what I've done to you. Lord knows I wouldn't have done it. But I guess if a man has to be haunted by memories of an enemy, it might as well be the handsomest enemy he's ever had.'

He stepped out, eased the door closed, ran a look down across that pewter-coloured yard to the bunkhouse, saw nothing to detain him and hiked on back to his drowsily waiting horse.

He rode back the way he'd come to the dim hills and never once looked back. It was in him to feel anger and resentment. Instead, he felt frustration and a kind of wilting sadness. This mood lingered until he'd climbed back around that fat haunch of hillside, struck the Fortier Pass trail, and wound on downwards to the plain below.

It was a benign night, unusually balmy for springtime Colorado's uplands, but perhaps that big old yellow moon had something to do with that.

He rode slowly, indifferently, most of his usual buoyancy drained out, which bothered him too, because always before he'd been one of those rare men who welcomed a fair challenge, who faced adversity head-on.

Where the first wafted scent of cattle came out to him he paused in his homeward ride to think, and in the end he decided he just wasn't up to all the prying questions old Stumpy, Art Cowan and the others would smother him with back at the wagon, so he dismounted where a fat little juniper cast its fat little dark shadow down a little slope, hobbled his animal, off-saddled, lay back and considered the big opaque sky.

The only recourse left now was precisely what Marshal Coleman, Ed Morrow, even Meredith Fortier, had warned him against trying. Break out through Fortier Valley.

The alternative was to go belly-up.

He envisioned the future and found it neither good nor bad. Men would probably die; he might even be one of them but this didn't occupy his thoughts very long. The thing which he must now do was get those cattle through Fortier Valley before he was stopped.

And he would be stopped, he knew that.

41

Meredith and Morrow might not do it, but Marshal Coleman with a bristling posse of perhaps fifty men could do it, and they would, so he *had* to be beyond Fortier Valley before that happened. Why? For the elemental reason that when Coleman arrested *him*, which Coleman would most certainly do, Art Cowan could still take the herd on north to the gold camps, peddle it piecemeal to those meat-craving glory-holers, then return to Denver with his pack-load of gold and bail Benedict out.

It might cost a small fortune. It probably would if Meredith had anything to say about it, or if the legal workings could put their clamps upon him, but still he'd have his fortune or at least as much of it as those people would leave him.

He sat up listening to a rider somewhere far off south-eastward. That horseman began to sing an off-key sad cowboy song to bedded-down cattle which meant he was one of Benedict's own men, so he lay back again with his calculating thoughts.

*She,* and probably that bewhiskered devil of an Ed Morrow, would put their heads together now, after his talk with her tonight, and they would put spies to watching his camp for signs of movement. He yawned. There was nothing to be feared from this. Idaho's wraith-like Indians had tried the same thing and he'd outwitted them. Anyway, he wouldn't move that soon. He'd let them sweat a little, then he'd hit that damned pass in the small hours of some gloomy night and by dawn he'd have stampeded his three thousand head so far down her valley he could be safely out of it before she could send to Denver for Jack Coleman and get him back up there with a posse.

He turned upon his left side, closed his eyes and slept. It helped, being a man of iron nerves. It helped a lot.

## CHAPTER FIVE

Stumpy had the breakfast well along. Cowan, Milt Stillwell and short, stocky, blue-eyed and straw-haired Johnny Emerson were squatting around when Hugh returned to the wagon-camp. They looked around as he eased down over at the rope-corral, put up his animal and dumped his gear. They went back to eating as he strolled on over to also eat, noticing as he did this that Tex Rathbone was not in camp.

Stumpy solemnly dished up fried spuds and meat, filled a battered tin mug with black java, and handed them over. He also said, 'Don't tell me, I can read it plain on your face. She said no, again.'

Hugh ate and drank and ignored Stumpy until the pleats were ironed out of his insides,

43

then he put aside the plate, the cup, and looked around. Cowan saw that look, mumbled that Tex was out making a survey of the cattle, and leaned back to quietly and patiently create his first smoke of the day.

'She said no,' Hugh stated, and watched their closed faces for reaction but there was none and Stumpy soon made it apparent why there was none.

'We sat around last night under that full moon figurin' your chances, an' we come to the conclusion she wouldn't soften up any.'

'That's clever,' Hugh murmured to them. 'Since none of you have ever talked to her, I reckon you boys just know women.'

Cowan blew out a bluish cloud, looked through it and said, 'It ain't exactly knowin' women that made us figure that, Hugh. It's knowin' human nature. Once a feller says no about somethin' an' has the time to justify what he's said to himself, the next time it's just that much easier to say no again.'

'Philosophers,' growled Hugh, rising up, twisting to mightily stretch and to afterwards run a palm over his beard-shadowed face. 'For thirty a month and found I get not only top cowboys, but sagebrush philosophers as well. Stumpy, don't use all that hot water on the dishes, I got to shave.'

Rathbone drifted in an hour later when the other men were loafing under the texas. There wasn't anything to do, which suited these tough men very well. They'd bucked rivers and forests and mountains in a rush to get this far. They could now loaf with every bit as much aplomb as the Indians used to loaf after one of their strenuous outings. Something in the uplands' winey, thin air did that to men; made them capable of prodigious exertions, then endless periods of idleness.

'Cyards,' called Stumpy, scuttling out of the wagon with their greasy playing cards. 'Poker for a penny, draw or stud. Who's in?'

Rathbone ambled over from caring for his animal, looked in, walked over to get a cup of java, and turned to watch Hugh finish shaving. He had a sardonic little expression down around his thin, long mouth.

'Hugh,' he said, 'we got watchers.'

Hugh and the others peered out where Tex was standing. Rathbone finished his java, flung away the dregs and dropped the cup into a bucket of greasy water. He strolled on over and flung out a sinewy arm. 'Yonder up in the hills near where the trail heads into the pass. I seen 'em when sunlight struck their metal things about a half hour back.'

Art Cowan drifted a look over towards the northward dark old hills. 'How many?'

'Don't know. Two, maybe three.'

Rathbone ducked under the texas, watched old Stumpy shuffle their cards, looked over at Cowan then on over to Hugh, and said, 'Sure pleasant people, these Coloradans,' and dropped down for Stumpy to deal him into the game. 'You know, when I was a kid down at Rio Bravo in Texas, when an outfit closed the range like they're doin' here, why we just sort of opened it again.'

Hugh stood a moment with his back to the others gazing north-westward along the foothills. Without turning around he said, 'We're going to open it, Tex, but not until the moon's lost a little of its brightness. Be pretty hard to get this herd up into the pass under a full moon without being seen miles before we had a chance to get down the other side.'

Rathbone nodded. Milt and Art Cowan craned around at Hugh. Stumpy and stocky Johnny Emerson took this announcement in stride without looking up from their card-hands. Emerson said, 'I never had no doubt of that,' and in the same breath he quietly said: 'Who can open, I ain't got anything but a one-eyed jack.'

Hugh left his place near the wagon's tailgate, came over and dropped down beside Stumpy. When the garrulous old cook looked testily up, uncomfortable about having someone watching over his shoulder, Hugh smiled and said, 'Just to keep you honest, Stumpy. Just to keep you honest.'

He never did join in the game and after a while he strolled over to look in on their horses. One big advantage to a rope-corral was that it could be moved twice a day providing the horses with fresh grass. Another big advantage was that as long as the grass remained close by, no one had to go very far to saddle up.

He later on walked out as far as the bisecting meadowland creek, found a wide place and took a bath, dried in the sun and kept covertly watching along the distant foothills. Once he saw the sharp, quick flash of sunlight off a round and polished glass surface. Someone over there in the rocks had a spyglass. He finished bathing, re-dressed, had a smoke out there under the warming sun, and acted as though he hadn't a worry in the world, or a suspicion.

Along towards mid-afternoon when they were all at the wagon Rathbone's keen eyes picked up something else of interest. 'Rider skirtin' eastward far out,' he said, showing where that horseman was over against the shielding hills. 'Now who would that be, I wonder?'

'That would be,' said Hugh quietly, 'one of the men from Fortier Valley headin' down to Denver probably with a message from Miss Fortier.'

'Message to who?' Art Cowan asked, narrowing out his straining gaze towards the distant, moving speck.

'I'd guess to the U.S. Marshal,' Hugh answered, also watching far out.

Rathbone grunted. 'She's scairt then, an' I

sure like that.'

'Not scairt, Tex,' corrected Hugh. 'Just preferring to let the law do her work for her, probably because she figures we wouldn't try to battle the law where we just might be willing to battle her.'

Lanky and youthful Milt Stillwell drawled, 'Hugh, with that big bay mare I could catch that feller before he even gets clear of the hills to the Fort Collins road. What say?'

Hugh shook his head. 'What'd we do with him if we had him, Milt?'

Stillwell didn't answer and the others had nothing to say about that either. They watched the Fortier Ranch rider swing southward out away from the mountains and cut diagonally down-country well away from their camp. He rode steadily, the way a man rides who has what he considers an important chore to perform.

They watched him out of sight and afterwards they rigged out and rode with Hugh to check the drift of their cattle. One advantage to desert country—where there was only one waterhole maybe every hundred miles, critters didn't drift far. In well-watered places such as Colorado and Wyoming, critters, especially steers with neither homing or herd instincts, could drift as far in two days by choice as a band of good riders could push them involuntarily in one day.

It was pleasant, doing this kind of work

where there was no strain, no sense of urgency, no need to rush here or there, so they talked back and forth as they rode along, sometimes joking, sometimes speculating on their future, always conscious of those distant watchers with their spyglass but never seeming the least concerned, never making any show of knowing that the men from Fortier Valley were spying upon them except to make a sly joke about it now and then.

The Idaho cattle were enjoying this rest after all those arduous weeks on the trail. They were neither disposed to drift very much nor rattle their wicked horns when riders passed by. It was good here in the dazzling sunshine hock-deep in emerald springtime grass with snow-water creeks to drink from. They would, as Meredith had said, put on fat.

As Art Cowan observed a trifle tartly, 'If there wasn't them other herds behind us it'd almost pay to lie over here a week or such a matter.'

And also as wry Tex Rathbone observed: 'There's always an "if". I figure life'd be pretty simple and smooth except for them "ifs".'

They returned to camp without Hugh having much to say. Stumpy was busy preparing barren-doe stew for supper so they left him pretty much alone, for if old Stumpy Crawford wasn't the best camp-cook in the West, at least he certainly was just as temperamental and touchy as the best cook

49

would have been.

They killed the remaining daylight hours moving their rope-corral to fresh grass for the night, and they cleaned up, fetched in full water buckets for the morning, and by then Stumpy was ready for them.

They ate and afterwards cleaned their dishes and gathered a fresh pile of buffalo chips for the morning fire, then they had that council which invariably followed suppertime at all wagon-camps when everyone was sprawled out replete and comfortable.

'Can't wait too long,' suggested Johnny Emerson, bringing out into the open what was uppermost in all their minds. 'If we do we'll lose out to them other herds.'

'Yup,' agreed Milt Stillwell. 'Feller doesn't mind too much workin' until his tail-feathers droop, so long as he isn't doin' it all for nothing. Let those other herds pass us by though, and it will have been all for nothing.'

'How'll they pass by?' asked Art Cowan. 'They can't use the Fort Collins road either, and they'll get bottled up behind Fortier Valley too, just like we are.'

'Could be quieter herds,' said Milt defensively. 'Could be quiet enough so'd they could be drove right alongside all those glory-holers out on the road.'

'In a bull's eye,' snorted Art. 'They don't raise no bottle-calves along the Snake River that I ever heard of.'

50

Hugh smoked and toyed with a cup of coffee and finally said over to Rathbone: 'Tex, you take first go-round tonight, only never mind night-herding the cattle. Head over into those foothills and see if our spies are camped over there or if they've pulled back over into their valley.'

Rathbone sombrely nodded, blew out a smoke ring and lazily got upright to stand a moment gazing over at Hugh. 'Anything else?' he said. 'If they're up there maybe I could sneak up an' bust a skull or two.'

'Not tonight,' said Hugh, knowing all of them were waiting for what he'd say next; had in fact been waiting all day for this pronouncement. 'Maybe tomorrow night or the night after that, but not tonight.'

Tex nodded and walked out where the land lay silvery-lighted and hushed. The others glanced around at one another and said nothing at all even though every one of them was now forming some careful thoughts. This was going to be a fight, they knew that. It was also going to be bucking the law. But every rangerider who'd come to manhood interpreting his own law according to his .4.5 and his personal feelings, more often than not considered that other law, that law of courts and books and settlements, a kind of interloping law. If it was necessary to go up against it, why then a man just loaded up, got into his saddle, and did what had to be done, and if afterwards he was outlawed, why so much for that. This was a big world, this land west of the Missouri and north of the Canadian. There were hundreds of men living very comfortably in it right now whose faces or likenesses had filled wanted posters years before.

But a man who weaseled out of his obligations, who failed not only those to whom his loyalty was unswervingly dedicated, but who also failed himself, just wasn't any kind of a man at all.

'How many riders she got?' asked Johnny Emerson in a too-casual tone of voice.

'Five I think,' answered Hugh. 'The rangeboss is a big black-bearded old bull-elk of a man named Ed Morrow. The others—well—they seem ordinary enough. Good riders and ropers. Nothing unusual as far as I've seen.' Hugh thought of something and said, 'They've been gathering for a brandin' bee over in her valley, which'll complicate things. It'd be a lot better if we could keep the herds separated.'

Art Cowan was indifferent about this. He said, 'We didn't pick the time or place, Hugh. If she's dead-set on a fight, why I expect she'll get the consequences.'

Cowan watched Stumpy flagrantly cheating at solitaire upon an old grey blanket. Stumpy was listening closely to all this but he wasn't entering into any of it. Milt Stillwell, sprawled with his shoulders planted half against a wagon-wheel also watching old Stumpy spoke up finally.

'Hugh, how d'you figure to work it?'

'Night after tomorrow the moon'll be less bright. It won't rise for two hours later. We'll head 'em up into the pass during that dark time. With a lot of luck we ought to be at the top-out up there or damned close to it by the time the moon finally comes up. We'll head 'em down. The minute they hit the valley floor we'll stampede 'em straight southward to that valley's lower end, then northward on up through the open country towards the Laramie Plains. And Art . . .'

'Yeah, Hugh?'

'The law'll be after us.'

'I expect it will.'

'Well, I'm going to drop back and let myself be taken.'

Cowan's head snapped up. So did the other heads. Hugh met their looks and nodded. 'They'll stop if they catch me, boys, and that's all the big lead you'll need to get 'em out of her valley and on up to the mining camps. Art, you sell 'em all then head for the U.S. Marshal's office down in Denver and bail me out.'

Cowan dropped his brooding gaze to the ground in front of him. For a while he said nothing, then he sighed and wagged his head and said, 'It's a good-enough plan, but I sure hope for your sake none of her riders get killed or you'll probably wind up dangling from an oak limb, Hugh.'

## CHAPTER SIX

They waited until ten o'clock for Rathbone to return, and when he didn't they drew straws as usual for their nighthawking and as one rode out to circle the herd, the others turned in.

This nighthawking wasn't so much to prevent the Idaho critters from drifting as it was to scatter manscent around in the night so any hungry wolves or lions or bears didn't get too bold. Actually, there were only two ways the cattle could drift anyway. They could head back down the trail until they struck the Fort Collins trace, and all the camp-fires and noise down there would deter them, or they could wander up into the foothills and perhaps strike on up Fortier Pass, but that wasn't too likely because the foothills were black stone with no grass, and even if they got up there it was a safe bet before they got down the far side into Fortier Valley they would be turned back by those spies up there in the rocks.

Milt Stillwell had the last watch. When he returned to camp just at sunrise Tex was riding with him. As they gathered to eat, Tex reported that he'd located the place where the men from Fortier Valley had kept their vigil, but they'd evidently pulled out ahead of sunset.

'That's the way it is with them shack-rat cowpunchers,' stated old Stumpy. 'Feed 'em at a table for six months and so help me Harry all they think of the full day-long is gettin' back to push their boots under that damned table again.'

Rathbone waited for Stumpy to finish then imperturbably said, 'There were three of 'em originally, from the sign, but two pulled out early, maybe in midafternoon, leavin' the last one to keep watch until just before sundown. And, Hugh—odd thing—one of 'em dropped this.'

Tex was holding out a little yellow ribbon tied in a full bow, and his tough eyes were close to smiling.

Hugh took the bow, recognised it at once and put it into a pocket. 'Hers,' he said, and lifted his cup of coffee.

'I sort of doubted it belonged to any of her men,' drawled Rathbone. Then he laughed aloud, something he very rarely did, which brought all those other interested faces around towards him.

'Hugh, you seen that spyglass-reflection yesterday?' asked Rathbone, still enormously amused about something.

'Sure I saw it. What of it?'

'Well, I got to piecin' things together, you see, as I poked around up there, and it come to me that you went out to the creek, stripped down and took a bath.'

For a hushed second they all sat or stood there by Stumpy's stone-ring figuring out this innuendo, then Milt Stillwell doubled over laughing. So did Johnny Emerson and Stumpy Crawford. Art Cowan sat there cross-legged, his coffee cup half-way to his mouth, looking straight over at Hugh, grinning.

Tex Rathbone's amused twinkle lingered on Hugh. 'I guess folks should get to know their neighbours,' he drawled. 'Only I'm not sure I'd want a female to know me *that* well.'

Hugh looked at them feeling high colour flooding up into his face. He grinned, shook his head and went on eating. He had nothing to say to this and the more he sat there dwelling upon it the more embarrassed he privately became. Damn a man who left his ranch to a girl anyway. There should be some kind of a law. Not just against girls but against them being allowed to own spyglasses, or ranches, or something.

Stumpy was gasping and dashing at laughter-tears in his eyes when Art Cowan, sitting opposite Hugh and looking eastward over Benedict's right shoulder, sobered them all.

'Riders coming from the east,' he said. 'Looks like maybe ten, fifteen of 'em.'

They hurriedly finished breakfast and spread out around their camp watching those oncoming men. Rathbone, who seemed to have the peculiar ability to make out detail much further than ordinary men could, called on over to Hugh saying, 'Twelve of 'em. They're armed for war and the heavy-set one out front's got some kind of shiny badge on his vest-front.'

Cowan grunted loudly and eased out away from the wagon where he'd been standing with one hand lightly lying upon a carbine. 'Her damned messenger got to town, I see. Hugh, this'll be your pappy's old wartime friend you rode down into Denver to see, I reckon.'

Stumpy growled something about disliking the notion of feeding perfectly good coffee to sheriffs and federal marshals and the like, but he too left his defensive position beneath their wagon and roughly pushed the big coffee pot back over the coals.

Those riders came on slowly and in all the immensity of empty land they seemed small, seemed insignificant. It took them another quarter of an hour to drift on into the camp and dismount. By then Hugh had recognised Marshal Jack Coleman. He didn't know any of the others but then he hadn't expected to; they were rough-looking men in checkered shirts. Some wore rangemen's dress, boots, spurs, neckerchiefs, and some wore the heavy, low boots and suspenders of miners. But every one of them was armed with a Winchester upon his saddle and a .45 in his belt.

Coleman gazed around, evidently to the men at Hugh's wagon, then he tossed aside his reins and strolled on over to coolly say, 'Good morning, boys. Good morning, Hugh.'

There was a little ripple of politeness from the rangeriders around their wagon and Hugh Benedict eased back his hat, walked over to draw two cups of Stumpy's oily coffee and offer one cup to Marshal Coleman. As Coleman amiably accepted the cup his faded, shrewd blue eyes drifted around the camp, out beyond it where red-hided cattle were distantly visible, and finally they flicked on up-country towards Fortier Pass.

Hugh didn't push things. Coleman would, he knew, say what he had to say in his own good time. Stumpy, Art Cowan and the others stood slightly apart from Hugh and the federal officer, eyeing those twelve posse-men out there who had made no move to come any closer.

'You've got a good camp here,' said Coleman, sipping coffee and watching Hugh with interest. 'Plenty of grass, water. Everything it takes to put tallow on critters an' keep riders content.'

Hugh smiled with his lips but not his eyes. 'It's a good enough stop-over,' he agreed. 'Even got mountains around it that cattle can't climb.'

'Unless of course they get a little help, Hugh.'

58

'What does that mean, Jack?'

'Well, there's Fortier Pass over yonder. Cattle could go up over there if someone was to show them the way.'

Hugh's smile turned sardonic. 'Is that what she's afraid of, Jack; that my cattle might drift over into her valley?'

'Not exactly, Hugh. She's worried about you helpin' them get over into her valley.'

'So she whimpered for help. We saw her man heading for Denver yesterday, Jack. It didn't take a lot of imagination to guess why.'

Coleman looked down into his empty cup. Hugh stooped to pick up the coffee pot and refill his cup but Marshal Coleman shook his head. 'No, thanks,' he said, and looked around for the wash-bucket, found it and dropped the cup into it. 'Like I told you the other day in my office, Hugh, she's got the law on her side.'

'Jack, listen to me. There's no other way to get this herd to the diggings. I can't use the road and we all know that. Not with half-wild Idaho cattle. I offered her two-bits a head crossing fee.'

'Yeah,' drawled Coleman. 'And she refused.'

'Two-bits is a generous offer, Jack.'

Coleman made a wry smile. 'She needs your two-bits about like I need trouble, Hugh. She's got more money now than she'll need for as long as she lives.'

'I know. She's dead-set against anyone else making money, Jack. Listen; we wouldn't be in

59

her damned valley but a couple of days. Three at the most.'

'It's a big valley, Hugh. You'd have to keep your herd in a trot all day to pass out of it in that length of time.'

'Then we'd keep it in a trot, but if we don't get up through there I'm going to lose a fortune.'

Coleman was unperturbed. 'It's a tough problem all right,' he conceded. 'That's why I came out here today. To ask you not to make it any worse by forcin' your way through.'

'Can you reason with her, Marshal?'

Coleman shook his head. 'I doubt it, but when I leave here I aim to ride on over into Fortier Valley.'

'Tell her if she . . .'

'I can't *tell* her anything, Hugh. All I can do is suggest. I'll do all I can.'

'Sure,' said Benedict, considering the lawman's unruffled calm. 'And if you go about like you're talking to me right now, you might as well save your breath, Jack, because being impersonal about this thing won't get you anywhere. I know; I've tried being nice to her. I also dropped a vague threat or two. I think she responded more to the vague threats.'

Coleman shook his head at Hugh. 'Don't threaten,' he said in a quiet, steely tone of voice. 'If you ever had much of a chance, believe me, Hugh, threats would kill it. Ed Morrow's a tough man; threats roll off him like

60

water off a duck's back.'

'I'm not dealing with him, Jack.'

'Oh yes you are. Maybe Miss Meredith's the owner, but don't ever kid yourself that she doesn't lean heavily upon big Ed in matters like this. You see, her pappy put a big store by Ed's ways and it just naturally follows that she does too. Whatever you told her went straight over to Ed Morrow. He'll be watchin' you like a hawk.'

Hugh twisted to also drop his empty cup into the wash-bucket. When he twisted back he said, 'What's the answer, Jack? Sit around here and lose everything?'

'No. It wouldn't be that bad anyway, son. You could peddle your beef at a fair price around Denver. We got a lot of hungry mouths too, you know, and so far there aren't enough ranches here to take up the slack.'

'Jack,' said Hugh evenly, 'I'm not interested in being a dirt-farmer, in selling my beef for a fair price. I'm a gambler. I've taken the biggest gamble of my life, and I took it to make one big clean sweep—one big killing by pushing my cattle straight up to the mining camps where beef'll sell for a dollar and better a pound. Now here I sit, kept from completing my drive with less than a hundred miles yet to go, by a girl who's got her back up against me for no real reason. What kind of a man do you think I am to sit around here and let everything I've sweated for go down the drain?'

'I know the kind of a man you are,' replied Coleman. 'I knew your pappy and you're his spittin' image, except maybe you're a mite taller and a mite handsomer. But the two of you come from the same pod in all the important ways, Hugh. That's why I came out here today; like I said down in my office, I don't want to fight you. Not just because your pappy was closer'n a brother to me in the war, but because I got no son of my own, an' if I *did* have I'd want him to be just about like you.' Coleman's pale eyes never wavered. His expression never changed and his voice was almost inflectionless in its iron resolve. Coleman only seemed like a pleasant, ageing man; he was actually as deadly and as resolute as a ton of black iron.

'So I'm here to tell you for the last time, Hugh—don't try it. Whatever you got in mind—don't try it.'

'I'm supposed to just sit here, Jack?'

'I'll talk to her. I've known her a long time. Since she was a little girl. I knew her pappy too.'

'What kind of a man was he, Jack?'

Coleman's expression changed for the first time. A swift, dark shadow passed across his face. His eyes grew distant and a little cold. Then all that was gone and Coleman shrugged. 'Like most of us; some good, some bad.'

'Would he have sat here, Jack?'

Coleman lifted a big hand, stroked his jaw

with it and because he was a truthful, candid man he gave an honest answer. 'No, he wouldn't have. But if he was here now, in your boots, son, I'd be standin' between him and driving these cattle over into Fortier Valley against her wishes. Against any legal property-owner's wishes. That's my job—to keep the peace; to prevent trouble an' to run down them as make trouble.'

'If you want to keep the peace and prevent trouble, Jack, you get her to let me trail on through,' said Hugh, and started to move away. He didn't get far.

'Hugh,' called Marshal Coleman softly, showing a deep vertical line between his gun-metal eyes. 'There could be a third way. I understand Ed Morrow's making up a herd to take down to Denver. At least her messenger said they were gathering and marking, and in the springtime that usually precedes the makin' up of a trail-herd to town.'

'What of it?'

Marshal Coleman looked off towards Fortier Pass which lay atop the divide between big Fortier Valley and this smaller, not-so-rich valley where Benedict's camp and herd were.

'It's pretty simple,' said Coleman musingly. 'The only way Fortier Ranch has ever brought herds down to Denver to the slaughter houses is out through this valley we're standin' in. That's why old Jules spent so much time and money broadening an' developing Fortier

Pass.'

Marshal Coleman brought his steady gaze back to Hugh. There was a heretofore lacking shrewdness pinching those faded eyes nearly closed now. 'But I reckon the smartest of us got blind spots. You see, this here little valley where you are is public domain. No one's ever homesteaded it.'

Coleman stopped speaking and watched Hugh. For a long time they steadily regarded one another without a word passing between them. Then Hugh gently smiled over at the marshal. 'Thanks, Jack,' he softly murmured. 'I'm indebted to you for this. Now then, where's the land-office in Denver?'

'South of my office three doors, son. And Hugh . . . ?'

'Yes?'

'If I was you I'd leave right now. They close along about six in the evenin'. But if you ride hard you can make it.' Coleman walked slowly over beside Hugh and glanced around. 'I'll spend the night up at Fortier Ranch. Tomorrow morning I'll be back down here for breakfast. You see, I got to protect the rights of all the property owners. You understand, son?'

'Perfectly,' said Hugh, and pushed out his hand. Marshal Coleman gravely shook it and walked away heading for his stiff-standing, patiently waiting possemen.

64

# CHAPTER SEVEN

Cowan and the others were mystified. They watched Coleman ride off with his posse and they afterwards listened to Hugh's plan, but as Stumpy said garrulously, 'Who the hell wants to own land this close to a danged town in the first place, an' in the second place he just ain't got the time to mess around gettin' involved with stuff like homesteadin'.'

Hugh explained, but first he sent Tex Rathbone out to saddle him that leggy bay thoroughbred mare in their remuda; she was the fastest animal they had. In fact, she had won them a sizeable chunk of money in some of the towns they passed by meeting all comers and beating them. She was a long-legged, ewe-necked, pointy-eared flighty animal not worth her salt at anything but running. However, at running, she'd never met her match.

'It works like this,' Hugh told them. 'Fortier Ranch is getting set to work their stock and afterwards make up their spring drive of saleable beef down to Denver.'

'That figgers,' agreed Stumpy, darkly scowling.

'And they've made their own private trail down through Fortier Pass to drive their herds to market.'

'Get to the point,' said Art Cowan

impatiently.

Hugh smiled at Art. 'If *I* owned the land below Fortier Pass and out here in this valley we're camped in, *she* couldn't drive through without my permission just like we can't drive through Fortier Valley without *her* permission.'

'Ahhh,' murmured young Milt Stillwell, and he broadly, delightedly, smiled. 'Stalemate.'

But Hugh shook his head. 'No. It'll give me the leverage I need. I'll give her my claim, to let us through.'

'She won't take it,' said Johnny Emerson. 'She's got her back up against us an' she won't take it.'

'If she doesn't,' said Hugh, 'then so help me I'll give this valley to the first fifty settlers I can find on the condition that they'll come up in here, fence off Fortier Pass, and never let one head of Fortier cattle come out this way.'

'Isn't there another way for her get out?' asked Cowan, twisting to throw a speculative glance up towards the far-away notch in the intervening hills.

'Not that's so convenient,' said Hugh. 'Otherwise her old pappy wouldn't have spent so much time and money developing Fortier Pass.'

Tex returned with the leggy bay mare. He stood phlegmatically listening while the flighty mare kept fidgeting, shooting her run-away pointed ears backwards and forward, rolling the cricket of her half-breed bit, mincing left and right and never quite standing entirely still.

Cowan said, 'She'll be fit to be tied, Hugh. Tell me something; did that rough lookin' old lawman tell you about this?'

Hugh nodded as he turned to take the reins from Rathbone. He lay a quieting hand upon the brainless mare's neck and soothed her in this manner.

'Yeah,' called over Stumpy, still sceptical that there could be a way out of their dilemma without resorting to guns. 'But suppose they won't let you homestead this here land; then what?'

But Hugh stepped quickly up over leather and threw them a loose wave and spun away in an easy lope, the thoroughbred mare fighting her bit to get more slack in the reins so she could run, which Hugh did not allow her to do.

Cowan stepped back, tilted his head to see the sun, to gauge the time and the miles ahead of Hugh, then he turned and slow-paced his way over under the texas. He was gazing far out towards that high pass from beneath their filthy old shading canvas, his thoughts alternately hopeful and dismal, and he didn't hear Tex Rathbone's soft call until it had been repeated twice over. Then he turned to look over near the camp-wagon's tailgate where the others were stiffly standing.

'What is it, Tex?'

'Visitors,' said Rathbone in a wry tone.

Cowan stepped back out into the golden brightness, hiked on up where the others were looking northward, and saw them. For a while he just looked, then his forehead ploughed up into a deep scowl and he said, 'Her whole damned crew from the looks of 'em.'

Shrewd, stocky, Johnny Emerson muttered, 'I don't like it. If you're gatherin' cattle you don't take no time off to take your whole blessed crew somewhere—unless it's danged important.'

Stumpy's reaction was different. He usually thought in terms of violence, for after a lifetime of sweat and blood, flashfloods, stampedes and gunfights, he invariably expected the worst. 'With Hugh gone you're in charge,' he told Cowan, 'and they got one more gun than we can muster.'

'I hope it doesn't come to that,' murmured Art Cowan, troubled and uncomfortable but not the least bit afraid. 'We won't make the first move, boys. We'll be friendly if it chokes us. Stumpy, make a fresh pot of java. Tex, you'n Johnny watch your tempers.'

Milt Stillwell, watching that band of bunched-up riders swing due south straight for the camp as soon as they were parallel with the wagon, said, 'Tex, ain't that big man out front got a black beard on him?'

'He has,' stated Rathbone, following out Milt's line of reasoning. 'He'll be this Ed Morrow we've been hearin' about. The ring-tailed roarer of Fortier Valley.'

Cowan, who was intently studying those approaching riders, said, 'How'd they miss the marshal?'

'They didn't,' opined dour Tex Rathbone. 'They saw him all right, an' the fact that they kept out of his way seems to me to be a right good indication that they *wanted* to avoid bein' seen by the law. Like maybe they got somethin' in mind they figured old Coleman wouldn't approve of.'

'Yeah,' breathed Stumpy, straightening up to his full height. 'Like they figured on maybe massacrin' the bunch of us.' Stumpy started away. He had a huge-bored old Sharp's buffalo gun in the wagon.

Cowan turned and swore. 'You do like I say, Stumpy. You make a fresh pot of coffee— damn you—and don't go near that wagon!'

The riders were less than a thousand yards away now. They had slowed their animals to a stiff walk and were coming on with their faces set squarely towards the wagon-camp. Cowan had time for just one final admonition to his companions before the men from Fortier Valley could hear him. He said: 'Remember; don't say a thing about where Hugh went or why. And eat crow if you have to so's there'll be no battle here. I think Hugh's goin' to win this fight for us without firin' a shot, an' we sure don't want to get into no battle that's already bein' won without bloodshed. Just

69

think of that; keep it always in mind. No matter what they say—keep quiet.'

Cowan's advice, like most reasoned-out advice, was good. The trouble lay not at all with his argument; it lay with the type of men he addressed it to. Johnny Emerson, for example, was a reformed outlaw. Milt Stillwell was a tough, laughing youth who'd never yet had the opportunity to prove himself against other tough men, and he had the hankering to do so. Old Stumpy was a born and bred fighter. He had thirty-one scars over his carcass from bullets and knives, and he was by nature a short-fused man. Tex Rathbone, the saturnine, long-legged, six-foot Texan, had never backed off from a fight in his life and at twenty-five years of age he was seasoned and testy and blindly loyal.

Even Cowan himself, despite his excellent advice, was not a hard man to roil. He weighed two hundred pounds and every ounce of it was bone and muscle. He had rusty red hair, a turkey-like red neck and the yeasty disposition which went with both. He had never been an outright troublesome man; he'd never had to be because his size and looks made all but the very bold and very reckless shy clear when his eyes flashed. Still, Art Cowan was a man with a quick flashpoint; he could perhaps curb his temper, but too much antagonism, too many slights or veiled insults would bring Art Cowan up fighting.

It took men like these to bring three thousand head of Idaho cattle through the mountains, over the plains and rivers and around the settlements as far and as successfully as these men had done it. Lesser men never would have been able to bull their way past the first obstacle.

But the men from Fortier Valley, particularly big old rough Ed Morrow, ruler of a dead man's range, were the same breed of lion. If there was much difference between these two bands when the Fortier Ranch riders drew rein at the edge of Benedict's wagon-camp, it was perhaps as Stumpy had noted: Morrow had one more gun.

He swung down and stood at his horse's head gazing across towards the wagon, across Stumpy's fire where the bandy-legged *cosinero* was suddenly extremely busy measuring out both coffee and water for his huge old blackened pot.

'Where's Benedict?' black Ed Morrow asked, not bothering to precede this demand for information with any of the common range-country greetings.

Cowan said, where he slouched over against the tailgate between Tex and rough-tough Johnny Emerson, 'Not here.'

'I can see that,' exclaimed dark-eyed and fierce-whiskered Ed. 'Unless o' course he's hidin' in the wagon. What I asked was—where is he?'

71

Cowan's red neck got redder and Tex's long-lipped mouth gently flattened. Between the two groups of grim-faced men Stumpy worked on fussing first with coffee then with his fire.

'All you have to know, mister,' said Art, 'is what I just told you: Hugh's not here.'

Morrow stood bitter-eyed and hip-shot, one hand holding his reins, the other hand hooked by one thumb in his shell-belt. 'That's too bad,' he said. 'I rode a long ways to see him.'

'Stick around,' said young Milt quietly. 'He'll be back.'

'When?'

Milt lifted his shoulders and let them fall. He didn't utter a sound.

Over behind Morrow his riders seemed relaxed, seemed ready to jump one way or the other way; to fight or simply mount up and ride off. So far there had been no clue which way they'd have to go, but they were watching.

'Maybe I can help,' said Cowan past stiff lips. 'I'm his rangeboss.'

'Are you now,' answered Ed, running a slow, bold look up and down Cowan. They were about the same size, those two rangebosses, but Morrow was easily forty pounds heavier and twenty-five years older. 'I don't reckon you can,' he eventually said in a slow, rough drawl. 'You wouldn't have the authority.'

'For what?' asked Cowan.

'To move this Idaho herd out of here.'

72

Cowan looked over at Morrow. So did his riders. Even old Stumpy, squatting at the fire, glanced up.

'Why?' asked Cowan.

'Because I said so,' shot back Ed Morrow.

Tex Rathbone made a little derisive snort and Morrow's black and hostile stare swung towards him. But Tex blandly smiled, saying, 'Hay fever; I get it every spring.' And kept on blandly smiling.

'I'd have to have a reason,' said Cowan, when this little exchange was past.

'You got one. What's your name, mister?'

'Art Cowan. What's yours?'

'Ed Morrow of Fortier Ranch.'

Cowan barely inclined his head in acknowledgment of this rough introduction. Morrow ignored that, did not reciprocate, and kept staring hard at Cowan.

'I just gave you all the reason you need, Mister Cowan. You move 'em because I said to. Does that suit you?'

Cowan didn't answer right away. He had this figured out now. Morrow didn't care whether they moved the herd or not. He was pushing for trouble. He'd come here to break up their camp or scatter their animals; anything he had to do to make them fight.

'Care for some java?' he mildly asked.

Morrow looked down where Stumpy was squatting and up again. 'No,' he barked. 'All I want is to hear you say you'll move this herd of cattle out of this valley.'

'Which way?' asked Johnny Emerson. 'Up through the pass?'

Cowan had heard the knife-edge of Emerson's voice and he spoke in ahead of Morrow, saying, 'Easy, Johnny, easy. I'll handle this.'

Morrow's bearded lips drew upwards to disclose his heavy, square white teeth. 'You could try goin' up that pass,' he said to Cowan. 'I'd like to see you try that, Cowan. But I don't give much of a damn which way you go with 'em, just so long as you go.'

'How much time we got?' Cowan asked, and Tex Rathbone swung to stare at him.

Morrow's black, fierce eyes shone now. 'That's better,' he said. 'You got about ten minutes.' He was silently laughing at Cowan now. 'Think you can do it in ten minutes, Mister Cowan?'

'No, and you didn't really come here to make us move anyway, Morrow. You came here for some other reason.'

'Did I? What other reason?'

'Fight?'

The men behind Morrow began to lose a lot of their slouched easiness now. The conversation had finally got around to the meat of things. There was a stillness to the roundabout air. The sunlight seemed sharper, the quiet deeper, the measured breathing of armed men shallower.

'That's right,' said Morrow shortly. 'But I came down here to get Benedict, not you fellers. He snuck onto Fortier Ranch last night and scairt Miss Meredith. Now us Colorado boys don't hold with intimidatin' women-folk, so we thought we'd ride down today and teach him some Colorado manners.'

Tex Rathbone twisted to gaze out over the range. He straightened back and said, 'Too bad he ain't here, Morrow. I'd like to put a little cash-money on the outcome of a shoot-out between you'n Hugh Benedict—or a fistfight either, for that matter. But now you not only get cheated out of both, but you also better get your fat gut into that sprung-seated saddle of yours and head on back where you come from.' Tex jerked a thumb over one shoulder. 'Take a look out there, old whiskers. Maybe you thought you ducked them lawmen, but you didn't. That's a federal marshal headin' up that posse. He was bound for your valley, but I reckon he got curious about so many skulkin' cowboys, and turned back. At any rate, if you're fixin' to start a war you'd better get at it. He'll be ridin' in here within five minutes—then you rough-tough Fortier Ranch men'll be out-gunned, out-numbered, and out-manoeuvred.'

Long before Tex had finished, the men from Fortier Valley had sighted those loping horsemen swinging along towards the Benedict wagon-camp from the yonder

75

foothills. It was while they were staring hard out over the dazzlingly-bright grassy range, Ed Morrow staring hardest of all, that old Stumpy raised up on his unsteady, bowed legs, holding that big coffee pot, and accidentally stumbled over one of his rock-ring stones falling ahead and pouring a gallon of hot coffee down the front of big Ed Morrow.

Ed let out a bellow and tried to jump away. Stumpy recovered his balance and looked round-eyed at the mess he'd made of Meredith Fortier's rangeboss. He immediately dropped the pot and drew forth a filthy old handkerchief to attempt drying off Morrow with, at the same time making a very solicitous clucking sound and muttering apologies.

Morrow's black eyes flamed and his right hand dropped. Thirty feet away Cowan and Emerson, Stillwell and Tex Rathbone also dropped their right hands.

'It was an accident,' croaked Stumpy, hopping about. 'I'm sure sorry, Mister Rangeboss. Pure accident, so help me.'

Ed Morrow spun around, jumped into his near stirrup, swung over leather and wrenched his horse around. He sunk in the hooks and broke away with his cowboys right behind him.

Stumpy stood looking after him still making that little clucking sound.

# CHAPTER EIGHT

'You dad-blasted little runt,' said Art Cowan to Stumpy. 'He'd have killed you for that. And done it softly, and reached out for his hat. I've heard it said that wasn't any accident and you danged well know it wasn't.'

Stumpy made a reproving chirp at Cowan and craned to watch Marshal Coleman ride up and step down looking out where Morrow and his riders were loping away.

'Welcome back, Marshal,' greeted old Stumpy. 'Come have a little fresh-made java.'

Coleman walked up and several of his possemen accompanied him. He looked at the others, halted squarely in front of Cowan and said: 'Wasn't that Ed Morrow and his boys from over the pass?'

'It was,' assented Cowan. 'And I'm damned glad you decided to come back and have another look around, Marshal.'

Coleman grunted, turned and stared far out where the Fortier Ranch men were hurrying along ahead of their own dust, making steadily towards Fortier Pass. 'Like that, eh,' he mumbled. 'You know, when we spotted them suckin' back into the foothills like they didn't want us to see them I sort of wondered if maybe it wasn't big Ed and he was up to something.'

Stumpy came bandy-legging it forward with a fresh cup of coffee which he insisted the marshal take. Then Stumpy, completely forgetting his earlier and uncharitable comments about all lawmen in general and this lawman in particular, made a big expansive wave at those middle-distance possemen.

'Sallie on up, boys,' he called out. 'Coffee for all hands.'

Coleman swished his coffee without immediately touching it. 'What did he want?' he asked Cowan.

'To fight, Marshal. He said we had to move our herd within ten minutes, but he didn't care about the herd. All he wanted was for us not to be able to do something he told us to do.'

Coleman sipped, made a face and looked around at Stumpy. 'What'd you put in this stuff,' he asked, 'bear grease an' lye-water?'

But Stumpy was busy filling more cups, and helping him was Milt Stillwell. Johnny Emerson and Rathbone sauntered over to also mix a little with the possemen. There was an air almost of celebration where fifteen minutes before there had been red death in the air.

Jack Coleman didn't say much for a while as the other men talked pleasantly back and forth. He seemed lost in thought. But after a little while he sauntered over beside Cowan and softly said, 'I doubt if Ed'll try that again. At least not today. But all the same suppose I

78

leave five or six of my deputies here to sort of discourage him if he should get the notion again.'

'Suits me,' said Art Cowan with a big, relieved shrug. 'I don't mind tellin' you, Marshal, for a minute there I thought all hell was goin' to bust loose.'

'Well, Mister Cowan, you did just right. Just right. All a man has to do when Ed Morrow's roiled up, is look crosseyed at him. That's all it takes. He's a big man on a short fuse.'

Coleman strolled over by Stumpy's cooking-ring, ticked off five men and told them to stay at the wagon-camp until he returned for them on the morrow, then he told the remaining seven men to drink up their coffee and get astride, that they were still going over into Fortier Valley.

'You'll be as welcome as a skunk in a bedroll,' opined Stumpy. 'Marshal; that big feller with the black whiskers looks like a gen-u-wine villain to me.'

Coleman and his men went out, got astride, turned to cast back a careless wave, then they loped off towards the north-eastward where mid-day heat was making the black-rock hills dance and shimmer under a pitilessly bright yellow sun.

Tex Rathbone joined Cowan near the texas and dryly said, 'Pretty savvy old devil at that.' He was referring to Marshal Coleman. 'He's one of them sly, quiet, tough-thinkin' old cusses who fool you every time, they act so mild an' all.'

'He can be anything he wants to be,' stated Cowan. 'From here on he's a pretty handy feller to have around, in my book.'

Stumpy got into one of his rare good moods when one of those possemen Marshal Coleman had left behind turned out to be a some-time bull-cook in the mining camps and offered to pitch in and help the old *cosinero* rustle up their mid-day meal.

Tex Rathbone and Johnny Emerson fell into conversation with two Idaho cowboys who had drifted over into Colorado, as one put it, 'Plumb by mistake because didn't no one tell us where the dividin' line was.' These four eventually wound up under the texas playing stud poker.

Milt Stillwell joined in gathering buffalo chips out a ways from the camp for Stumpy's cooking-fire with another young cowboy, and these two kept each other laughing recalling how, when Coleman had ridden up earlier, each was afraid the opposite side might open up and start a battle.

Cowan made a smoke, lit up and considered Fortier Pass first, then the overhead sun. It was slightly after mid-day. With a tail-wind behind him, Hugh should be just about in sight of Denver by now.

'Hey, Art,' Johnny called from under the texas. 'Come sit in. It's a friendly game for a

80

penny a hand.'

Cowan looked around. His camp was relaxed and comfortable. It was good to hear men laugh again, after what he'd been through this day. 'Sure,' he said, and walked on over dropping and grinding out his cigarette on the way.

After they'd eaten, some of the men rode out to inspect the herd, several other, fresh hands, took over the poker game, and a few, like Art Cowan, just tossed aside their hats, lay down on the wagon's off-side where a little thin sheathing of shade was coming out, and snoozed. There was no reason to do anything else, but even so Cowan's right eye opened from time to time, rolled up and around, then closed again. He was having some difficulty forgetting the fierce face and belligerent black eyes of Ed Morrow, and no matter what, he had no intention of being caught flat-footed by that old he-devil again.

In this quiet way the day passed. Along towards evening when Stumpy was at work making supper, garrulously reciting the tribulations which had beset them since they'd first strung out their herd over in Idaho, pointing it eastward towards Colorado, to his new friend and helper at the cooking-ring, the riders returned from the herd and everyone squatted around to eat supper.

It was another of those unpredictably balmy springtime evenings with the sun dropping

81

away reluctantly so that daylight lingered almost until eight o'clock, and afterwards, because Coleman's possemen had their blanket-rolls aft of their cantles, each man sought out his own place to bed down.

Cowan put Tex Rathbone on the first watch and detailed Milt Stillwell to the second go-round, but an hour before Milt was to get up Tex heard a horse coming along through the soft darkness and went around gently awakening everyone.

It was Hugh, but if it hadn't been, if it'd been someone from over in Fortier Valley, he'd have got quite a reception. There were nearly a dozen armed men silently following out the sounds of the ridden horse with their drawn guns.

Hugh put the bay mare into their rope corral. Until he did that though, there wasn't a sound at the wagon, but afterwards, since no one else would set himself afoot, Cowan called softly to Stumpy to poke up the fire and put the coffee on.

Hugh walked over, saw that bristling camp, those additional guns in the night, and halted. Cowan walked out to him saying, 'It's all right. These here are some of Marshal Coleman's men.' Cowan related what had happened. He even told of Stumpy spilling hot coffee over Ed Morrow. Hugh took all this in without saying a word. He went over and wearily dropped down at the fire where the others silently, watchfully, joined him. Stumpy gave out the coffee again and Hugh, after one big swallow, looked up.

'It's mine, boys. I've got the papers in my pocket.'

Milt Stillwell whooped in boyish triumph while the other, older men, were just as pleased but in a more subdued way. To the possemen, who had been hearing all afternoon what Hugh was up to, Tex Rathbone dryly said, 'I reckon that fixes her little red wagon.' Tex's meaning was amply clear. The possemen dutifully nodded and accepted their cups from Stumpy.

'It may fix her little red wagon,' one of the possemen opined thoughtfully, 'but she sure ain't goin' to thank you any for fixin' it.' This man waited until some of the other knowledgeable locals were nodding over this observation, then he added to it, saying, 'One thing I learnt a long time ago about the Fortier outfit—you cross 'em an' all hell breaks loose.'

Another posseman, also a cowman, said, 'Mister Benedict, you just bought yourself a king-sized headache, for as soon as Ed Morrow hears they have been tricked, especially by an outsider, he'll come out of that there valley like a bloody-hand bronco buck Injun.'

Hugh looked up at those sober men and he said softly, 'Marshal Coleman's been impressing me for several days now with the fact that his job's to keep the peace. If *she* can

83

use the law for her ends, what's to stop us from doing the same thing?'

'Nothing,' stated Johnny Emerson with loud emphasis. 'Nothing at all.'

But Tex Rathbone, with his dry and somewhat pessimistic outlook, shook his head. 'What these boys're tellin' us is that law or no law we got us a tiger by the tail.'

'That's right,' said that first posseman with a strong nod of his head. 'When a feller gets Fortier Ranch by the tail he dassen't hang on an' he dassen't let go.'

Stumpy grunted disapproval of all this. 'How come everyone to always flinch when folks mention the Fortier outfit?' he demanded. 'Let me tell you boys something: This here trail-herd-outfit ain't a bunch of strict pansies either, y'know. We've already ridden over an' through our share of trouble, just gettin' this far.' He put his rheumy old eyes around that gathering at the stone-ring showing puffed-up indignation. 'Let me tell you fellers from Denver something—if old black-whiskers thinks he's goin' to put his arms around *this* outfit and wrestle a little, he'll damned soon find out he's got his arms around a sack full of deer horns.' Stumpy glared around, his neck bowed and his back stiff, but no one challenged him about this so in the end he became deflated and sat over there prodigiously yawning. 'I'm goin' back to bed,' he eventually announced, got up and stamped

84

away from the fire-ring over to his pallet under the wagon.

Gradually the others also drifted away until only Art Cowan and Hugh Benedict were left. Art toyed with his empty cup waiting for Hugh to speak, and when Hugh did not, Art quietly said, 'Well, do we still try pushin' 'em through or don't we?'

'No. We'll go over and tell her about this land-claim and offer to trade it for passage.'

'Yeah, I figured that much,' said Art. 'But what I'm wonderin' about is—what if she still says no?'

Hugh, who hadn't been altogether idle on the ride back, said, 'In that case we'll take 'em through tomorrow night, Art,' and raised his tired eyes towards Cowan. 'And of course that'll mean we're right back where we were before I rode in an' filed on this land.'

'Yeah. Outlaws the minute we bust down into her damned valley. Well, Hugh, whatever comes of this, can't no one decently say we didn't *try* to do it the right way first.'

Hugh flung away the dregs from his cup and put the thing aside as he rocked forward, rocked back, then jack-knifed up onto his feet and stood there looking into Stumpy's little dying fire.

'That probably won't be a hell of a lot of consolation, Art, if some of us get shot, or if I wind up in Coleman's jailhouse. But regardless, you do as I outlined before, if we have to break through her ranch. You keep the herd moving, get well clear of Fortier Valley, don't bother going back for strays. Just push on up to the diggings and peddle the beef. Then fetch the money back down to Denver and bail me out.'

Cowan also stood up. With the small fire between them they looked at one another for a long moment. They were equal in size and equal in toughness, and after having survived all they'd been through together, they were also equal in respect for one another.

Cowan said quietly, 'Don't worry. The boys an' I'll sell the beef an' be back to get you.' He smiled with his tough-set lips but not with his eyes. 'An' I don't reckon they got a stout enough jail in Denver to hold you once we set our minds to gettin' you out.'

Hugh smiled at his rangeboss. 'See you in the morning. By the way, did Coleman say he'd be coming back this direction?'

'Yeah. Said he'd spend the night in Fortier Valley and be back here for breakfast.'

'Fine. See you then.'

Cowan watched Hugh move off and privately thought Benedict looked damned well wrung-out.

# CHAPTER NINE

Marshal Coleman got back to the wagon-camp but not when Benedict's crew and those possemen expected him. Not, in fact, until long after they'd finished breakfast, because Stumpy habitually arose at five, served up breakfast by five-thirty, and Coleman with his riders didn't come into camp until close to ten o'clock.

He met Hugh over at the rope-corral where Cowan and Tex Rathbone were ironing out the last details of the private plan they had for the coming dark hours after this portentous day ended. Art and Tex nodded at Coleman and drifted on back to the camp where Coleman's newcomers and the others were all talking and standing around waiting for Stumpy to feed them, a chore Stumpy ordinarily would have bucked at like a bay steer simply because it was an iron-clad rule that if riders weren't around when chuck was served, they took up their belts a notch and waited until the following meal. But Stumpy, with his townsman-helper, made an exception here.

Coleman wore a long face and he kept eyeing Hugh askance. He finally said, 'She was as unrelentin' as a stone wall.'

'Yeah,' breathed Hugh softly. 'I honestly

didn't expect much else.' He fished inside his coat and drew forth a legal document. 'This is the claim-paper to the valley we're camping in, Jack.'

'You got it, eh,' muttered Coleman, looking disinterestedly at the paper. 'Hugh, there's somethin' here I can't quite put my finger on.'

Hugh put the paper away and looked over at Jack Coleman. 'Morrow hit the camp yesterday,' he said. 'But you knew that. I'd guess whatever it is that's bothering you has its root in Morrow's mind more than hers.'

'No,' contradicted Coleman, scowling. 'That's just it—it doesn't have. Oh, Ed's fired up against you. No one'd deny that. But that's not it.' Coleman lifted his perplexed, faded blue eyes. 'What's passed between you'n Meredith?'

Hugh looked into those puzzled old eyes and said, 'Nothing, Jack. Like I told you yesterday morning, I tried flattery and I tried threats. Neither of 'em worked.'

'No, no,' muttered the lawman. 'It's more'n that. What did you *do* to her?'

Now Hugh began looking puzzled. 'Do to her? What the hell do you mean by that, Marshal? I didn't do anything to her except try an' talk my way through her valley. What I'd *like* to have done was up-end her and use a willow switch on her, but I didn't, of course.'

'Now you listen to me,' said Coleman, the perplexity leaving both his face and voice.

'You've done *something*. I've known this girl since she was in pigtails. I figure I know her about as well as anyone does in this country, and I've never seen her so dead-set against something before in her life. I tried reasonin' with her. I even hinted that if she persisted in keepin' you bottled up out here, I couldn't be responsible for what you might do.'

'What'd she say to that, Jack?'

'Well. You'll wonder about this. She asked me if I knew your folks.' Coleman paused to lift his eyebrows. 'Now that had nothin' at all to do with what I was discussin' with her.'

'What'd you tell her?'

'That I served with your paw in the war. That he told me your maw died when you were born. She asked about your paw. I told her frankly about him.'

Hugh removed his hat and scratched his crinkly black hair, replaced the hat and kept watching Marshal Coleman with some doubt and some wonderment. 'What did all that personal stuff lead up to, Jack?' he ultimately asked.

Coleman lifted both arms and dropped them. 'Damned if I could figure it out. That's why I come to the conclusion that this here isn't just a matter of bein' afraid your two herds might get mixed up over in the valley; that it isn't simply a matter of her stickin' to her family's policy of no-trespassin' in Fortier Valley. It's something personal, Hugh. It's got to be something between you'n her.'

Benedict stood there gazing at Marshal Coleman saying nothing. He had also felt that, when he'd been in her house night before last, but he couldn't define why it should be like this. Surely she hadn't been able to read his mind, and that was the only thing she could have been indignant about, his private and secret thoughts concerning her.

She'd affected him every time they'd come together as no other woman ever had, but, even if she knew this, which she couldn't have because he'd never told her, it should be flattering to a woman; it shouldn't make her dead-set upon starting a shooting war with him.

He gently wagged his head. 'I'll ride over today and offer her a trade, Jack,' he said. 'I've got this land-claim like we figured, which'll cut her off from her usual route from the valley down to Denver. If she'll let me trail through I'll sign it over to her.'

Coleman nodded absently. 'I thought of mentioning that last night when we were havin' supper at her house. But since I had no way of knowin' you'd even get the land, I didn't dare mention it.'

'That's all right, Jack. I'll do it today.'

'Hugh? What do you figure to do if she still refuses?'

Benedict gazed over into those wet-iron old eyes and said, 'Be better if you hadn't asked

90

that, Jack.'

Coleman began wagging his head. 'Don't try it, son, or we'll be right back where we started from—set against one another. Me with the law, you ag'in it.'

'Well; let's cross that bridge when we get to it, Jack,' Hugh said smoothly. 'Right now I got a lot of ridin' to do if I aim to be back over here by sundown, so I'd better get going.'

'There's not that much of a hurry.'

Hugh, in the act of turning towards the roped-in saddle animals, looked over one shoulder and cynically said, 'Yes there is. Morrow won't get the chance to bushwhack me in broad daylight. But I wouldn't bet he couldn't try it in his own country after dark.'

'Pshaw,' scoffed Marshal Coleman. 'You're readin' Ed Morrow wrong, son. If he comes after you again it'll be straight up an' face to face.'

From over by the wagon Tex Rathbone sang out bringing both Benedict and Marshal Coleman around. 'Two riders comin',' said Tex. 'Look yonder towards the foothills below Fortier Pass.'

Hugh looked, spotted the moving specks and put a saturnine glance over at Coleman. 'Maybe I won't have to make that ride after all,' he said. Then raised his voice. 'Tex, is one of those a woman?'

Rathbone looked, was silent almost a full sixty seconds, then he called back, 'Yeah.'

Marshal Coleman stroked his jaw, drew downwards his thick brows and muttered under his breath, 'I wish to hell I knew more about women. Last night after supper out on her veranda she told me plain as day she never wanted to lay eyes on you again as long as she lived—an' here she now is, ridin' right up to your camp.'

But Hugh wasn't watching Meredith any longer because it was now possible to make out the unmistakable heft and sinister black beard of her riding companion. 'She's in lousy company,' he said to Coleman. 'Jack, I want your word about something; if Morrow gets tough you'll stay out of it.'

'Can't rightly do that, Hugh. But he won't get tough. I read him the riot act at their bunkhouse last night about comin' into your camp yesterday spoilin' for trouble.'

'Jack, I respect your judgment, but I didn't just roll out from under a boulder either. That Morrow is one of those men we've both seen around before. When someone looks at him wrong or happens to say the wrong word, he's ready to let go.'

'Sure-'nough,' agreed Coleman, his craggy old features hardening slightly. 'But there's somethin' you don't know, son. Ed Morrow and I have tangled before. He won't force no fight where he sees me standin' around.'

'Then he'll probably swell up, turn purple, and bust a blood-vessel, Jack, because I'm going to make them that offer of this land for passage through.'

The marshal and Hugh strolled on over towards the wagon where nearly twenty interested, curious men were standing around watching those two riders grow larger as they neared the camp. There was scarcely a sound anywhere around. Even old Stumpy wasn't moving, for a change. Art Cowan gave ground as Hugh and Marshal Coleman walked up, but except for looking around at them Art was motionless too.

While Meredith was still a hundred yards out Hugh saw that her great wealth of blue-black wavy hair was caught up at the nape of her neck with one of those small ribbons. This time it was red and bright and it complemented her colouring. She was wearing a dark split skirt, ankle-length, made of some rusty dark material and she had on a rich tan blouse that was immaculately crisp. Her feet and ankles were encased in soft dark boots and both her spurs were silver inlaid; they sparkled in the sunlight.

Her expression towards all those admiring men was untroubled and impassive; she seemed to see only one or two of them.

At her side Ed Morrow wasn't wearing the same levis and shirt he'd worn the day before, which Stumpy did not neglect to notice and secretly smile about. He had on one of those Hudson's Bay blanket-coats riders in the uplands frequently wore to keep out the cold, and because it was now warm this told those watching, silent men at the wagon that Ed had been in the saddle before sunup, which was enlightening.

'Probably waited for her up at the pass,' murmured Cowan aside to Hugh. 'Had to see what was goin' on down here.'

When Meredith reined up gazing over the heads of the men straight at Hugh, Morrow swung down, reached for her reins and held them as she also dismounted. Morrow was also staring coldly past to the place where Hugh and Art Cowan, and Marshal Coleman stood.

She walked ahead through that silent phalanx of waiting men and halted near Hugh. He felt that fierce pull again; she drew him against his will.

'I learned something interesting this morning,' she said tonelessly, and flicked a cold glance at Marshal Coleman as she said this. 'A rider arrived at the ranch who said you'd filed a claim on this valley, Mister Benedict.'

Hugh said nothing for a long moment. She'd very effectively thrown him off-balance with this pronouncement; had robbed him of his ace-in-the-hole. Marshal Coleman cleared his throat and glanced around. There was astonishment on Cowan's face, on a half-dozen other faces.

'Why?' she asked Hugh, watching his face

94

closely. 'To retaliate, Mister Benedict? Ed thinks you did that so you can prevent my herds from moving down across this little valley to Denver. Is that right?'

'Only if you make it necessary, ma'am,' said Hugh as he fished inside his coat and brought forth his land-claim paper.

'If I make it necessary; what does that mean?'

He held the paper out to her. 'You can have this to keep or tear up the second you give me permission to cross Fortier Valley.'

'I see,' she murmured, hardening her spirit towards him, facing him with eyes that showed swift cruelty. 'Blackmail.'

'No'm; a trade. I told you the other night how it was with me, and you know by now I can't stay here much longer. Reasoning with you didn't do any good. Appealing to you didn't either.'

'Neither did the threats, Mister Benedict, and neither will this threat.'

Hugh slowly returned that paper to his pocket. He looked past to where Ed Morrow was standing, his black eyes full of wrath and stubborn hatred for Hugh. Then he dropped his eyes to Meredith and said, 'Being vindictive never hurts the right people, Meredith, and as I told you before—you're the last person on earth I want to fight. But if you still won't listen to reason, or even to an appeal, why then I still have another ace up my sleeve.'

'Yes?' she inquired coldly. 'And what is that, Mister Benedict?'

'You can prevent my crossing Fortier Valley.'

'I definitely mean to do just exactly that.'

'And I will prevent you from ever bringing another herd down through here on the way to Denver.'

'How, Mister Benedict? You won't stay here and prove up on this land.'

'That's right, ma'am. But I can find fifty squatter-families who will, and I aim to give each of them a parcel of this land with the written stipulation that they never, as long as they hold any part of this land, allow a Fortier herd to come down here from Fortier Pass.'

Ed Morrow took a quick, harsh step forward, his bearded lips twisted to roar out. Jack Coleman, evidently expecting just exactly some such demonstration as this, barked sharply, 'You—keep back where you are, and don't you open your damned mouth. Not a single word, Ed. Not a one!'

Morrow, struck head-on by that biting voice, hesitated, glared at Coleman, and gradually lost some of his fire. But the hand holding the reins to Meredith's horse, was white at the knuckles from straining, and Morrow's fierce black eyes burnt with fire-points of cold fury.

Meredith, throughout this little episode, had not removed her eyes from Hugh, and after one brief glance, he did not look away from her either.

'I underestimated you,' she said in a knife-sharp quiet tone, to Hugh. 'But it's not going to be that simple for you, Mister Benedict. You see, yesterday I sent one of my riders scouting down below Denver, and there are two more Idaho herds pushing up this way. They'll be here within five days. In fact, they'll probably arrive here just as all that gold-rush traffic out on the Fort Collins trace is gone by. *They* have nothing to lose but *you* have. Five days is all I have to wait, Mister Benedict.'

He watched her beautiful mouth close against him. He quietly said, 'Is it worth all this, Meredith? Do you want to ruin one stranger that much?'

'Begging, Mister Benedict?'

He solemnly shook his head. 'Wondering is all. Wondering what could make so lovely a woman—so black inside.'

'You'll have five days to figure it out,' she said, and turned away from him, walked back over to Ed Morrow and faced around to say, 'You may ruin my trail to Denver, but I can blaze another. I can out-wait you and I can out-smart you, Mister Benedict. You're a clever man, but cleverness has never been enough. It also takes boldness.'

Hugh did not walk out to her. None of the other men moved either although Johnny Emerson and Tex Rathbone looked white and furious enough to do something rash. Even

97

Stumpy and young Milt Stillwell were keyed-up to violence.

Marshal Coleman was the only one who sauntered ahead, offered his hand, and afterwards said up to Meredith Fortier, 'I don't know when in all my life I've been so disappointed in anyone, Meredith.'

'For not being soft, Marshal; for not letting one opportunist ride rough-shod over me?'

'No, Meredith. For not showing the good sense your father would have shown.'

'He wouldn't have allowed this—this—profiteer, through the valley either, Marshal.'

'You're wrong, honey. Dead wrong. Old Jules wouldn't only have let him through, but old Jules was a good judge of real men. He'd have tried to keep him in the valley as well.'

Coleman stepped back and did not nod his head as Meredith turned, and with black-faced and frustratedly furious big Ed Morrow at her side, went loping back the way she'd come.

Cowan eased over beside Hugh and whispered, 'Still go through tonight?'

Hugh said: 'Yes. But act natural until Coleman takes his posse and heads for home.'

## CHAPTER TEN

Marshal Coleman, though, didn't take his posse and head for home. He sat around

98

Benedict's wagon-camp with a stubbornness that eventually convinced Hugh he had no intention at all of leaving.

Tex and Art Cowan came out to the rope-corral to mention this to Hugh and to say they couldn't possibly throw down on twelve men and hold them under their guns while also rounding up their herd for the push over into Fortier Pass.

Hugh knew this and gave an annoyed retort to those two. Then he went over where Coleman was quietly smoking in the shade and said, 'It's getting late, Jack.'

And Coleman said right back, 'Later than you think, son, but not so late you couldn't try it tonight.'

Hugh walked away. The other men of his riding crew became edgy and subdued. Even the possemen became infected by this strained atmosphere until Cowan came over and wagged his head at Hugh, saying, 'Too late now to get the job done even if they were to saddle up an' ride out right this minute. We're goin' to have to hold off at least until tomorrow night.'

'He's deliberately doing this,' said Hugh, referring to Marshal Coleman, sitting over there in the shade of their texas relaxed and smoking. 'He smells something.'

'Well . . .'

'Pass around the word, Art. Nothing doing tonight. Tell the boys to play a little poker if they want to, and relax. For now, it's a dead issue.'

Hugh stepped away and started out towards the rope-corral. Cowan let him get fifty feet off before he called softly out to him. 'Where you goin'?'

Hugh turned. 'To make one last appeal to her.'

'That's foolish,' said Cowan. 'Old black-beard'll be lyin' in wait up there some place. He'd give a year off his life to get his fingers around your gullet.'

Hugh didn't argue. He didn't, in fact, say anything. He simply went his way, caught a fresh horse, led it out of the corral and rigged it out. Cowan watched him do all this, sauntered solemnly out and waited until Hugh swung up, then Cowan said, 'Hugh, you could damn well get killed tonight. Anyway, by now it ought to be plumb clear she's never going to change her mind.'

'One more try, Art. We can't do anything tonight anyway.'

'Yeah? An' what if you get shot? Listen; you better at least let me ride along.'

'You stay here. One man can get around that pass without very much trouble; I know. I did it once before. Two men'd make too much noise. Anyway, if someone's going to get shot there's no point in both of us getting it. And Art—if I'm not back by tomorrow night, and everything else is in your favour—take the

100

herd through.'

Cowan stood there big and darkly scowling, his expression firmly disapproving, but he inclined his head to indicate that he would do as he'd been told. But the moment Hugh swung and went riding off into the gathering dusk, Cowan hiked straight on over to the texas, caught Coleman's attention and crooked a finger at the lawman.

These two paced out into the night a hundred yards before Cowan jerked his thumb backwards saying, 'Hugh's gone over into her valley for one last appeal, as he put it.'

Coleman wasn't as surprised as Art seemed to expect. He considered this announcement, hooked his thumbs in his shell-belt and kept squinting off towards Fortier Pass, which was gradually fading out in the gloomy dusk. Finally Coleman said, 'Hell,' with monumental disgust, and brought his gaze back to Cowan. 'You ever been in love?'

Cowan's jaw sagged. It took a moment for him to recover from the shock of this seemingly totally irrelevant question. 'What a tomfool question,' he exclaimed.

'Well, have you?'

'What's that got to do with it?'

'I wish I knew,' said Coleman. 'That's why I asked you. Cowan, you look like a sensible man. You know what I've been tryin' to piece together around here all afternoon? Why two such ordinarily sensible people keep on actin' so entirely irrational as Meredith Fortier and Hugh Benedict.'

Cowan's leathery face slowly formed a grimace. 'Love?' he whispered. 'You sayin' them two are in *love* with each other, Marshal? Good gawd; if ever I seen two people hate one another with everything in 'em to hate with— it's my boss and that long-legged, black-headed girl.'

'Yeah, but that's just my point, Cowan. Now listen to me for a minute, then tell me what all this means. Night before last she told me she never wanted to see Hugh Benedict's face again as long as she lived. Then this morning, s'help me, here she comes to spit'n scratch at him. An' now you take Hugh. He keeps sayin' she's the last thing on this earth he wants to fight—then he gets all keyed-up to fight her.'

'Hell, Marshal, Hugh's got no choice. He's got to fight her.'

'Naw,' said Coleman disdainfully. 'I don't think so. All Hugh's got to do is catch that handsome young heifer, take her by the horns, and make her ride right along beside him right up through her damned valley—and not a man-jack among her riders'd lift a hand to interfere. Not even Ed Morrow.'

Cowan stood there staring. 'Hostage,' he breathed. 'My lord, Marshal. You hit it square on the head. Why didn't someone think of that before? Why didn't you tell Hugh about this idea?'

'Why?' said Marshal Coleman. 'I'll tell you why, Cowan. Because I've already pulled his chestnuts out'n the fire once in this duel, an' I'll be damned if I can risk gettin' involved any deeper. But besides that, Cowan, I'm a federal U.S. lawman; I got no right at all suggestin' things like hostages. That's plumb against the law.'

Coleman squinted through the deepening gloom at Cowan. He reached up and scratched his chin. He turned and looked off towards night-hidden Fortier Pass. Cowan also turned to gaze in that direction, but Cowan's expression was vital now, full of fresh energy and resourcefulness. As he turned away he said, 'Reckon I'd better go check the horses before turnin' in,' and walked away.

Coleman shrugged, let Cowan get clear across the wagon-camp into the yonder darkness before he moved, then he sauntered down where several of his older possemen were sitting in the warm night sporadically talking, smoking their pipes, and he sank down near these men to speak swiftly and softly in such a way that the gamblers around the wagon where a hot poker game was in progress by coal-oil lamplight couldn't hear.

'Jake, Mike, Whip. You fellers get up from here, walk far out an' around, get your horses saddled and wait out a half mile for me. Not a sound now, and don't tell anyone what we're up to.'

103

'That,' dryly commented a grizzled miner knocking dottle from his little stubby pipe, 'won't be hard to do, Jack, since don't any of us have the least idea what you're up to.'

Marshal Coleman straightened up, lingered on the wagon's dark side until those other men had also arisen and slipped away, then he strolled around where the noisy poker game was in progress. Cowan wasn't there. He watched the game for a while, drew one of his possemen aside, spoke briefly with this man, then lounged on out towards the night-hidden rope corral and there made a count of the saddles belonging to Benedict's crew. Two were missing. One belonged to Hugh and obviously the other one belonged to Art Cowan, who would by now, he thought, be a mile out and still loping along in his big effort to overtake Hugh and pass along the suggestion of holding Meredith Fortier hostage for as long as it would take to pass the Idaho cattle through Fortier Valley.

Coleman straightened up from counting those saddles and softly frowned. There were, he was convinced, all manner of damned fools in this world, and up until this night he'd always personally held that the biggest fool of the lot was the one who mingled in other folks' affairs, which is exactly what he'd been doing now for the past half-hour, and if he didn't get someone killed or hurt, it would enormously surprise him. But on the other hand, if he'd ridden away, which he'd have had to have done no later than the following morning, he knew Hugh Benedict well enough to know Hugh was only waiting for him to take his possemen and leave so he could storm up over Fortier Pass, down into the valley, and shoot his way through if necessary, which would, in Coleman's carefully considered opinion, cause infinitely more harm than what Coleman himself was trying to do.

He also went over the whole mess in his mind again, while he stood out there watching his own private animal come out of the corralled beasts to reach over and sniff at him, all the disconnected and unlikely things which had occurred to him this afternoon as he sat there under the texas quietly smoking and knottily thinking, and it came out the same: she was irresistibly as attracted to Hugh as he was to her. But they were both made of the same kind of pig-stubborn iron, and they'd each be damned and beaten bloody before either of them would surrender to the other.

Well, Coleman thought, if that wasn't love, then he didn't know what love was. He caught his horse, led him out of the rope-corral, rigged him out, got quietly aboard and quietly rode out into the north-eastward night.

'Of course,' he explained to the horse. 'Never havin' been married or even what you might say was really in love, the Good Lord knows I sure am no authority on the subject.

Still an' all, if there's some other explanation to this war these two are cookin' up against one another, I'll be double damned if I can figure it out. Now if it was two *men*, I'd have the right answer right off: a man doesn't live to reach my age and not know his own kind. But what we got here is totally different, horse. What we got here is . . .'

'Is that you, Jack?'

Coleman snapped his lips closed and squinted ahead where several riders sat. 'It's me,' he said.

'Well, who you talkin to?'

'My horse,' blandly answered the lawman, and that miner out there said, 'Oh,' as though everyone carried on involved conversations with their saddle horses, which as a matter of fact all men much alone did, and he turned to ride along with the marshal.

'North-eastward?' the burly miner asked.

'Yeah. Up Fortier Pass.'

'We figured as much. That feller Art Cowan went by just as we got out here.'

'Sure,' said Coleman. 'An' before him, Hugh Benedict also went up that way.'

They passed quietly along through the total darkness speaking a little now and then but otherwise quiet, otherwise resigned to another long night astride.

'Sure dark out,' said one of them.

'Perfect night for stampedin' cattle up through the pass,' said another man. 'Marshal, you wouldn't suspect Benedict of havin' anythin' like that in mind, would you? That wouldn't be why we killed this whole cussed day loafin' around his wagon-camp, would it?'

Coleman turned and gazed at the speaker. 'Why, Mike, what a suspicious mind you got,' he said reprovingly.

There was a slight ripple of wry laughter at this and the burly man riding along beside Coleman fished out his stubby little pipe, carefully filled it, lit up behind his shielding hat, snapped the match and puffed a moment before he said, 'What'll the others say when they discover we're gone, Jack?'

Coleman lay both hands atop his saddlehorn and smiled. 'They'll say good riddance, an' thank gawd Marshal Coleman didn't made us all ride out with him.'

For a mile after that none of them had anything to say. The countryside was steeped in a total hush, a total blackness. The moon wouldn't be up for a while yet, which hadn't been overlooked by Marshal Coleman. It had occurred to him long before that Hugh had also taken that belated moonrise into consideration in his plan to invade Fortier Valley once more. Ed Morrow, or whomever else might be keeping a sharp vigil up atop Fortier Pass, would be very effectively limited in his sightings by all this formless night. Unless someone rode straight up the pass and was heard riding over rock, at least seven men were going to get over into Fortier Valley this night undetected.

Coleman knew this country as well as anyone else did, even including big Ed Morrow. Cowan he had a few doubts about; to his knowledge Art Cowan *didn't* know the pass. But Coleman, the excellent judge of men, didn't worry too much. Art Cowan would find a way around through the lower-down hills exactly as he also knew Hugh Benedict would.

The land began to tilt, to pitch and buckle. Coleman rode as much by feel as by instinct. He guided his companions unerringly around the base of Fortier Pass, out along a fat sidehill, and very neatly avoided the pass altogether.

## CHAPTER ELEVEN

The moon arose near ten o'clock, half of it lopped off but the remaining half enormously ancient and yellow-lighted. Every open space that filtered brightness touched down, there were lengthy shadows. It was, in a way Hugh could not define, an infinitely sad night.

He came out around and down into Fortier Valley exactly as he'd done two nights earlier, and he encountered cattle and horses along the creeks as he'd also done before, but by the time he was approaching the Fortier place he felt a difference in the night. It seemed as though something solemn was out here with him.

He halted a half-mile out when this feeling was strongest and carefully considered the onward lighted buildings. Something or some one was out in the night with him. He was certain of that so he turned off, passed far out of his way to gain the seclusion of that little finger of forest he'd left his horse tied in before, gained this shadowy place, dismounted and stood back in there for a long time, just gauging the night.

Then he saw the lanky silhouette straighten up upon the yonder porch of Meredith Fortier's main ranch house, stretch, yawn, take up a carbine and amblingly stroll once down the porch and once back.

Morrow evidently was taking no further chances on Benedict getting in to see Meredith. He left his horse, considered the best way of getting around the house, and started moving through speckled shadows. Sometimes the moon was a hindrance, sometimes it was a help.

He got to the edge of the house from around the back, listened, heard that cowboy around there make his little round again, sidled along until he could flatten near the front juncture of the side wall and the front wall, drew forth his .45 and stood as quiet as stone.

The sentry came ambling along again, each footfall measured in cadence and heavy of tread. When the man halted at the porch's extreme ending Hugh allowed him a moment to look around, to turn for the walk back, then he stepped out, stepped up behind the cowboy and swung his gun overhand. After that he was instantly involved in catching that falling body and in preventing the man's Winchester from striking the floorboards and making a racket. He was successful both times, tossed the man's carbine out into the dusty yard and used both hands to settle his unconscious adversary into a comfortably sitting posture against the front wall. The man's face, once Hugh pushed aside his askew hat, proved to belong to that same non-smoking cowboy he'd talked to up at the pass two evenings before.

For a moment he awaited any indication that others might be abroad. When he was quite satisfied that this was not so, he stepped on past, approached Meredith's front door, raised his fist and softly knocked. Inside the parlour, someone passed along in front of a lamp briefly interrupting the steady outward flow of yellow light, then the door opened and without a sound Hugh pushed on past the startled girl, eased the door closed and leaned upon it.

He smiled. She was as startled by this unexpected appearance as he'd expected her to be. She started to speak, to castigate him, her eyes sparking, but he put a finger across his lips and gently wagged his head at her. She instantly checked herself becoming no less stiff and indignant, but quiet.

His smile deepened. 'Thanks,' he murmured. 'There isn't anyone out there. I just wanted to see if you really knew how to obey an order.'

'You,' she said, in a low, savage voice, 'get out of my house immediately or I'll open that door and call for Ed.'

'In a minute,' he replied. 'First I've got something to say, and something to do.'

'It won't change a thing. Not a thing, Mister Benedict. Nothing you could say or do . . .'

'Meredith, you're the most thoroughly handsome woman I've ever seen in my life.'

She wasn't as startled at this pronouncement as she might have been, but she nevertheless stared at him unsmiling or unable to finish her statement.

'I'll give you that valley I filed on whether you let me through your valley or not.'

'I wouldn't take it from you. Now you get out of . . .'

'One more thing, then I'll go,' he said, suddenly stepping well forward from the door. He caught her unprepared, caught her by the waist and pulled her up against him. He dropped his head in a swift swoop, found her mouth and insistently burnt her with his kiss.

She didn't resist but neither did she soften

111

against him. She stood ramrod-stiff tolerating the rough pressure of his mouth for as long as he kissed her, and when he afterwards raised his head, straightened up and looked down into her eyes she said in a choked, strangled voice, 'I'll have you killed for that,' and broke clear of him.

He was no longer smiling. He said, 'Your privilege, ma'am, to try an' have me killed. But let me tell you, bitter as that kiss was, it'll carry me over a lot of years, just in memory.'

'Even though I didn't give it; even though I despised you every moment of it?'

He nodded. 'If I have to be satisfied with a lot less than it should've been, I'll be that satisfied, Meredith.' He moved back by the door again. 'To tell you the truth I didn't expect it to be any different than it was.'

'Oh you didn't, didn't you!'

'No. Because I think you're one of Nature's ironies; a beautiful woman with ice-water for blood, no heart at all, and a black will to you that would torment a man for as long as he lived.' He lifted the latch behind him but did not turn, did not pull the door inward just yet. 'The best you've got to give is a picture of you standing just as you're standing now. Lovely in the lamplight; a sight for a man to always carry with him. But it ends right there. You're not a full woman at all, Meredith. You're a mockery.'

She moved swiftly and swung, her eyes

ablaze, her cheeks red with wrathful blood. He caught her hand with no particular effort and threw it back at her.

'That was expected too,' he told her. 'And now you'll call for Morrow. Well—go ahead. I owe him something too.'

'He'd cut you down like a mad dog.'

Hugh stepped over, pulled back the door and showed her that golden-lighted yonder yard. 'Call him,' he said.

But she didn't. She didn't even walk past him to the doorway. She stood there staring up at him with her expression turning troubled and suddenly afraid.

'Call him,' he reiterated. 'You've made a lot of big talk. Now back it up. Call Morrow over here. I'll give him an even break right here in front of you. And I'll kill him the same way— right here in front of you.'

She still didn't move, so after a moment Hugh shrugged and eased the door closed again. Now his eyes were showing scorn. 'Where is all that fury now?' he asked. 'Meredith, there's just one thing in my mind worse than a coward—that's a bully. Female or male, I've got no use for bullies. You said down at my camp this morning that it'd take more than a clever man to take my herd through your valley. It would also take a bold man. Well, I reckon you were right.'

'You'll never get them through,' she said, her voice pitched low. 'Bold or not, I'll bury

113

you if you try.'

'All right. But dig more than one grave because I've studied your crew, and let me tell you something: my four riders, even old Stumpy, my *cosinero*, are a match for anything you've got on your payroll. As for Morrow, I'll attend to that one myself. He came down to my camp hunting trouble. Well, now I'm here in *his* bailiwick for the same reason . . . Meredith?'

'Yes.'

'Come over here.'

She didn't move but her eyes steadily widened as she read his intent.

'I said come over here.'

'No.'

He released the door, took two long steps and she backed away from him, but awkwardly, as though she were too confused, too unsure to move rapidly. He caught her in the centre of the room by both shoulders and held her at arms length for a moment, not roughly but not tenderly either. He said quietly: 'Outside on your porch is an unconscious man. Let the hurting end there.'

She could look up and see his tawny eyes and the hard cut of his dark head against backgrounding lamplight; could see the sharp flaring of his nostrils with each indrawn breath. 'Times are changing, Meredith. Men like your paw and Ed Morrow belong to an earlier day. If you're confused and bitter because of the

114

challenge I represent, learn to bend a little with the wind of change. I promise you that if you don't learn to do that—you'll go under.'

'You'll do that to me?' she whispered.

He shook his head. 'Not I. I'm only one man. Only the first man to challenge you. There will be others by the dozen as time goes along. You can't whip us all and sooner or later Ed Morrow and men like him will go under too, because they're too old and set in their ways to change. But you're not—unless you're too stubborn to change, and if that's the case I pity you.'

He drew her gently to him. She didn't resist. He dropped both his hands from her shoulders and softened towards her, lowered his head and brushed her lips with his mouth. She didn't step away. She let him do that and she afterwards gazed up at him out of eyes turned almost black. He saw in the depths of her stare mysterious things and in a tender voice he said, 'Think about the things we've discussed, Meredith. Think about them hard. I'll wait at my camp to hear from you.'

He crossed to the door, opened it and stepped through. Off on his right a heavy moan came almost like a sigh through the otherwise stillness, then a voice gently said: 'Steady, feller. Real steady right where you're standin'.' And he heard a gunhammer click backwards. He didn't move except to roll his eyes around to where the lanky shadow

115

detached itself and stepped closer, peering into his face.

'Be damned,' said his captor. 'I sort of wondered if maybe it wasn't you who cracked Will over the head.'

'And now you know,' said Hugh, picking out a second tall shadow moving soundlessly in behind the first one and for a moment believing this was Ed Morrow because the second shadow was not only tall but was also broad and thick-made.

His captor gently waggled his head back and forth. He seemed almost impersonal. 'Got to hand it to you, Benedict, you sure don't give up easy.'

'I don't give up at all, cowboy. I can't afford to.'

'That's too bad because Ed'll want to lynch you for coming back an' botherin' Miss Meredith again. He's already said as much.'

'That's what he had in mind when he visited my camp this morning, I suppose.'

The cowboy stepped still closer. Hugh recognised him finally. He was the soft-talking man who had rolled a smoke up in the pass when he and another Fortier Ranch rider had lingered behind when Meredith and Morrow had ridden away several nights back.

The cowboy said, 'Naw, all Ed wanted with you this mornin' was to punch some sense into your skull. To inspire a little scare in you for the Fortier outfit. But now, well, let's walk on over to the bunkhouse and find out.'

'What's the hurry?' asked that second silhouette further back in the gloom, and the Fortier rider stiffened, his eyes growing round with astonishment. 'Ease down the hammer of that gun, mister, and hand it to me behind you.'

Hugh's brow furrowed. He knew that voice, it belonged to Art Cowan, but what was Art doing here; he'd distinctly told Cowan to stay at the camp and Art had agreed. Cowan had never before disobeyed him.

The Fortier cowboy slackened off his hammer, hefted his gun for a thoughtful second as though debating exactly what he ought to do, then pushed the gun straight out behind him.

Cowan took the weapon, pushed it into his waistband and struck downward. The Fortier rider crumpled making a little rustling sound as he settled all in a heap upon the porch planking.

Cowan said: 'Listen, Hugh: Coleman give me an idea, but you only got a couple of seconds to make up your mind about it. He said Morrow and these others wouldn't try to harm us if you was to have Meredith Fortier ride through her valley beside you when you bring the herd through. Coleman said they wouldn't dare start a fight as long as she was a hostage.'

Hugh scarcely let Cowan finish before he

117

said, 'Where's your horse?'

'Back in them trees where I came across your animal tied to a sapling.'

'Then let's go,' said Hugh, and started quickly along the porch.

'But wait a second,' protested Cowan in a loud whisper as he stepped out after Hugh. As he passed that other man who'd been hit over the head he happened to glance downward. That one was reviving; was in fact reaching clumsily for his hip-holster as Cowan came even with him. Scarcely missing stride Cowan bent, plucked away this man's .45 and gave it a hard toss out into the yard.

Hugh moved rapidly back up into the little spit of trees. Cowan came even with him up there still protesting this empty-handed withdrawal. As they were riding along keeping to the trees for as long as this was possible, he said, 'It's a sound idea, Hugh. They'd be afraid of starting anything if we had her along.'

'I don't like it,' Hugh responded. 'I never liked hiding behind skirts, Art. I'm surprised at you considerin' it.'

Cowan turned silent after this rebuke and rode along saying no more until, near the foothills again, he hissed and held up one hand.

Hugh also saw them. Five horsemen slouching along towards the rearward dark buildings, riding directly across the big meadow out in plain sight. He sat and studied those men and when they were well past he eased out again homeward bound. 'Coleman,' he said. 'He followed you, Art.' In a reproving tone he added: 'I'm surprised at you.'

Cowan looked uncomfortable and obviously felt the same way. He had nothing more to say all the way back to their dark and silent camp.


## CHAPTER TWELVE

Tex Rathbone and young Milt Stillwell were out with the herd at seven o'clock in the morning full of Stumpy's heavy pancakes and black java. They saw the horsemen coming through Fortier Pass by their scuffed-up dust and Tex sent Milt back to warn Hugh and the others.

Those possemen Jack Coleman had left behind knew at last that they'd been deliberately left behind, which didn't please them too much, but what they resented even more was Coleman's manner of sneaking off in the night like that, as though, as one of them grumbled, he didn't trust his own deputies.

But all that changed the moment Milt loped in with his information. Johnny Emerson and Stumpy, at the stone-ring sipping coffee and having a smoke, lost all their easy indifference and went quickly for their guns. Hugh, also hearing Milt's announcement of riders coming, finished shaving and quickly dressed as Art Cowan, who had been leaning there arguing the advantages of taking a hostage, pushed upright off the wagon's sideboards and told Milt to go after Tex and come back to camp before they were both cut off out there. Milt spun his horse and loped away.

A posseman coming around from under the texas where the everlasting poker game was in progress, said tartly that Hugh's men acted like everyone who rode up was set on making war. Hugh looked after this edgy man but said nothing back.

Milt loped back saying he hadn't had to ride far because Tex had been drifting closer. But he came alone. 'He says to tell you,' Milt informed Hugh, 'that it's only the marshal, an' that he'll stay out there a little while to make sure them Fortier Valley fellers aren't also slippin' up on us again.'

Hugh finished stuffing in his shirt-tail, reached for his weapon-belt, flung it around, buckled it, bent down to lash the tie-down thong, and afterwards strolled over where both his riders and the possemen Coleman had left behind were standing soberly watching that string of horsemen wind out of the yonder dark foothills and boot their critters over into a long lope heading straight for camp.

Cowan turned and called: 'Stumpy . . . ?'

'Yeah, I know,' came back the immediate growl. 'More coffee. You got any idea how much coffee we've used up lately?'

Cowan either didn't know and didn't care, or he did know and still didn't care, because he ignored Stumpy to resume with the others watching Marshal Coleman's dusty approach.

While the federal lawman was still a hundred yards out Hugh thought he detected a slouched and gloomy posture among Coleman's riders which could not be entirely attributed to saddle-weariness. After dwelling upon this for a moment he said to Cowan, 'Something's wrong, Art.'

Cowan nodded without looking around. He too had detected that dourness among the approaching men.

When Coleman came up, halted and stepped down, he flexed his legs, looked over at Stumpy's coffee pot, hooked his reins upon a wagon-spoke and with little more than a glance at all those watching men over by the tailgate, struck out for the fire. His riders also got down, but they went ahead to mingle with the others.

Hugh intercepted Coleman as the marshal was pouring himself a cup of coffee. He said, 'What's wrong, Marshal?'

Coleman finished pouring, looked straight over at Hugh across that tin cup and said, 'I got a signed warrant in my pocket for your arrest, son.'

'From—her?'

Coleman shrugged. 'She wouldn't see me.

121

Ed Morrow signed it. It's for trespassin', assaultin' two of his men—one of whom identified you—and for house-breakin'. It was that house-breakin' that made me snort. But Ed's right; he's got the law on his side.'

Coleman drank deeply, tossed down the cup and let off a big sigh. He glanced over where Stumpy was standing stiffly staring at him. To the *cosinero* he growled, 'Don't look at me like that; I don't make the laws, I only get paid to enforce 'em.'

'Since when's tryin' to prevent bad trouble a crime?' demanded irate Stumpy Crawford. 'You know yourself Hugh's been bendin' over backwards to keep the damned peace, Marshal.'

Hugh waved a hand to silence old Stumpy, so the cook turned and went angrily stamping on over where Cowan and the others were.

'I'll have to take you in, Hugh. 'Course, it's only a formality. You can post bail an' be home again by nightfall.' Coleman yawned and sadly shook his head. 'It's partly my own damned fault,' he mumbled. 'I had a theory—it didn't pan out.'

'This is a nuisance objective of Morrow's,' Hugh said. 'He can't come up with anything better, so he figures to be spiteful.'

'Well, yes. It seems that way all right. Still, I've got to honour his complaint.'

'Why wouldn't she see you, Jack?'

Coleman's bushy, shaggy brows drew

together. 'Damned if I know. She didn't even come out of the house while we were there. I sent a man to fetch her; she told him Ed Morrow would transact this business for the ranch.' Coleman lifted weary shoulders high and let them drop. 'You think you know about people, then they do something you never expected 'em to do. I reckon if that proves anything, Hugh, it proves you never really know folks at all.' Coleman's face smoothed out, turned curious. 'What happened between you last night?'

But Hugh didn't feel like discussing this any further. He was busy with his private thoughts and he turned away to head over towards the rope-corral, Coleman watched him go without moving. Even when Cowan walked up and said, 'What the hell, Marshal,' old Coleman kept watching Hugh out there in the middle distance and ignored Cowan for a while. Then he quietly said, 'He's under arrest. Morrow swore out the warrant. You heard all this from the others, Cowan.'

'But what's his point, Marshal?'

'Maybe spite. Maybe something else. Like I was just tellin' Hugh, a feller never really knows people. Well, it's time I was gettin' back to town anyway. Do me a favour—tell my men to get mounted up.'

Coleman walked slowly out where Hugh was rigging out a horse, stood thoughtfully quiet for a time, then he said, 'I don't know what Morrow's up to, Hugh, but let me tell you something: don't give 'em any more ammunition to use against you by havin' your boys try anything rash while you'n I are down in Denver.'

Hugh turned, shot Marshal Coleman a cold look, stepped up over leather and said, 'Better get your men rounded up, Jack. We've got a lot of miles to cover.'

Coleman nodded but kept gazing up at Hugh's tough-set expression for a moment longer before he blew out another big sigh and walked off.

Tex Rathbone came riding in, got down close to where Hugh was sitting his saddle waiting, and said in an undertone, 'I just heard. Milt told me. When'll you be back?'

'As soon as I can post bail.'

'Anything you want me to pass along?'

'Yes. Tell Art to stand ready. The minute I get back tonight we put the herd up the pass and down through her damned valley.'

Tex looked up and mirthlessly smiled. 'Sounds just right,' he murmured. 'I been wonderin' how long we was goin' to go on playin' hide'n seek with that bunch of pot-lickers over there.'

Hugh saw Jack Coleman waving at him over where he and his riders were astride and ready to depart. He said, 'Tex, keep an eye peeled,' gigged his horse and rode away.

Art, Milt and Johnny Emerson stood like

stone statues watching Hugh ride off with Marshal Coleman. Out where Tex was lingering at the rope-corral, Rathbone gravely watched this departure also, but where the others seemed troubled Tex didn't; he actually looked pleased.

The heat was beginning to build up. It was a little after eight o'clock with a crystal-clearness to the upcountry air. Dust came to life under the hooves of the posse's animals and where they passed a scattering of Colorado's distinctive, wild little columbine flowers, Jack Coleman said, 'I think it's a delaying tactic, Hugh. I been figurin' all the way back from her valley—it's got to be some sly notion they got to delay you another couple, three days until those other herds catch up.'

To Hugh this sounded reasonable, and yet in the back of his mind there was some other little elusive thought moving around. He couldn't pin it down; when he tried it skittered away.

'But you know,' went on Marshal Coleman conversationally, as though he was having some difficulty puzzling this out, 'I've known Meredith since she was a little kid. Yesterday she disappointed me, but this morning up at her place when she refused to even see me—it just didn't seem at all like her.' Coleman looked around. 'Could it be that something happened up at her house last night between you two?'

'Yeah,' said Hugh flintily. 'Something happened all right. I kissed her, Jack, when I should have taken off my belt and whanged hell out of her.'

Coleman's eyes widened but he didn't say anything. They rode along down through the rough-shouldered pass where, as long as the air stayed clear, they could distantly make out the Fort Collins road running northward as straight as an arrow.

An hour later when they were angling off southward parallel to that road but staying well clear of its endless traffic, one of the possemen's horses half threw a shoe. There was a slight delay while this offending object was forcibly tugged completely off and the horse's owner resumed riding on towards town with a barefooted horse.

By the time Denver was well in sight those men, including Marshal Coleman, who had been in the saddle without rest most of the night before, were succumbing to that warm sun across their backs and also to the rocking, rhythmic gait of their horses. They drowsed along fitfully sleeping.

Coleman jerked erect when the morning northbound stage whirled by clatteringly and laying a broad streamer of dun dust in its wake. 'Run somebody down,' he growled, narrowing his eyes. 'Some day they'll enact a law against drivers hittin' it up to ten miles an hour like that, by golly.' He cleared his pipes, spat out dust, and removed his hat to swipe at sweat upon his forehead. 'Hugh, I had a ridiculous notion yesterday.'

'Yeah?'

'Yeah. I kept tryin' to figure out why you'n Meredith were like flint and steel every time you were together. She'd look at you, you'd look at her, and the damned sparks'd fly. I figured it out that you two were in love with one another.'

Hugh's head flung around. 'You what?'

'Well hell, boy, there had to be some kind of an explanation. It just isn't natural for folks to despise one another without ever givin' cause.'

Hugh looked on ahead where the teeming town was coming out to them and said nothing. Coleman gazed ahead too, but he wasn't viewing the town so much as he was facing one direction with his eyes while thinking in a quite different direction with his mind.

'And you said you kissed her.'

'There's a difference, Jack. A kiss doesn't mean a thing unless you get kissed back.'

'Oh. I see.'

'Do you? That's more than I do.'

They entered town from the north and were immediately assailed by Denver's one constant and identifiable factor—dust. Every road and trail was churned to powder by the clamouring horde of goldseekers hurriedly fitting out for the northward trek, and dust was everywhere, in the air, upon the store-fronts, wherever a man put his hand he encountered layer upon layer of dust.

They got to Marshal Coleman's office where the possemen were released and sent on their individual ways. Then Hugh had to wait until Coleman stabled his tired horse before the marshal accompanied him through a heaving tide of excited humanity to the local courthouse, an ugly timber building in Denver's diminishing plaza, where Coleman duly handed over his completed warrant, requested bail, and leaned with both tired shoulders hunched forward over the counter beside Hugh until the officious clerk came back and said, 'Twenty dollars, Marshal, an' he'll be arraigned sometime next month. I'll have to let you know exactly when. Our court calendar's so full now we couldn't possibly fit him in.'

Hugh passed over the twenty dollars, got back a hastily scribbled receipt, walked back out of that foul-smelling building and put a sceptical look over at Coleman.

'All that riding, all that damned delay, just for that.'

Coleman nodded sympathetically. 'It's the law, Hugh, it's the law.'

They strolled back where Hugh's horse was tied at the rack before Coleman's dingy office, and there they shook hands. Coleman said, with a wry little wag of his head, 'I still don't understand what's in her mind.'

'I'm not worried about her,' said Hugh, unlooping his reins. 'I'm wondering what Morrow's got in mind.' He stepped around beside his animal with the hitch-rack between them, looked back and said, 'Jack, hasn't it struck you yet that Morrow'd know all I'd have to do in town was post bail then head on back?'

'Well yes; just as we were enterin' town it came to me he'd know that.'

'Then think this one over too,' said Hugh flatly as he toed into the stirrup, rose up and settled across leather. 'All Morrow probably wanted was to get me away from my camp for a few hours.'

Coleman's tired eyes gradually came to a bright, intent sharpness. 'To hit the camp?' he asked.

'Or the herd, Jack. I got to thinking about that a while back. What other reason would he have for pulling something as ridiculous as havin' me run in for that silly list of charges?'

Hugh was reining around when Marshal Coleman said swiftly, 'Wait. I'll get a fresh horse at the livery-barn. Hugh, wait!'

But Hugh was already riding back out of town the way he'd just come in.

# CHAPTER THIRTEEN

The mid-day sun was building up its daytime shimmery heat by the time Hugh cut away from the Fort Collins road towards that narrow pass leading into his valley. Near the entrance he encountered two wagonloads of gold-seekers making camp. One of those rough men straightened around where he was bent over shoeing a big sorrel mare to carefully watch Hugh lope past. When Hugh returned this long look the miner threw him an amiable wave and went back to work.

Two of these men were inside the valley through the pass. Both had shot-guns and were astride big, awkward-footed harness horses bareback. As Hugh came along they turned to uncertainly watch him. One of them, the more direct of the two, kneed his animal over to intercept Hugh and when they both halted this miner, a burly but quite young individual, said in a slow Virginia drawl, 'Hope we aren't steppin' on anyone's toes by huntin' in here, mister. If it's private land just say so an' we'll ride back out.'

'No, go ahead and hunt,' said Hugh. 'But all I've ever seen this low down is a few sage hens.'

This thick-set man broadly smiled in relief. 'We'd settle for sage hens,' he said. 'Feller gets powerful weary of salt pork.' Then he said something that electrified Hugh. 'We was goin' to ride on closer to those distant foothills figurin' on maybe sightin' a b'ar or deer, but awhile back it sounded like there's already some hunters over there. They sure-'nough was bangin' away too.'

'Gunfire?' asked Hugh quickly.

'Yes, sir, and a heap of it too.'

Hugh hooked his horse and left those two sitting there looking dumbfoundedly after him. He hadn't travelled a half mile before he saw a red-flashing tide of heaving backs and clicking horns heading straight towards him. The ground underfoot began to gradually reverberate from the panicked stampede of his Idaho cattle.

*Morrow!* he thought. *Getting him arrested had only been a ruse to weaken his crew!*

Without another thought concerning the men from Fortier Valley he whirled his horse, sunk in the hooks and raced back towards those two miners on their big draft horses. They saw him wildly riding down upon them, hauled around and stared.

'Stampede!' he yelled at them. 'Get through the pass there's a stampede coming!'

Both the miners frantically wrenched their big animals around and belaboured their sides with gunbarrels. Even so, Hugh shot out through the pass's stone shoulders a hundred feet ahead of those men, spun off to the right

131

and cried out to the other miners at that wagon-camp.

Men came tumbling out of those two wagons, nearly a dozen of them, some armed and wary, some simply astounded by this apparition which burst into their camp.

Hugh slid his horse, sending a shower of gravel over the closest men. 'There's a cattle stampede coming towards the pass. I warned your friends beyond the hills; they'll be out any second now. But stand clear or those cattle'll grind you to dust.'

An aged, leathery-faced and rawboned miner with a Springfield rifle in one mighty fist raised this gun and gestured with it, at the same time roaring an order at his companions. 'Come on, boys, run for it. Get up to the pass an' give 'em help.' As this man broke ahead in a run he bawled backwards: 'Fetch your weapons!'

Hugh turned his horse to stop this madness. Whether those miners knew it or not the moment they appeared in the pass they would be run over and ground to a pulp. But that leathery-cheeked old rawboned man was leading his companions, not straight into the pass, but up to it alongside the rough stone bulwark alongside it. Hugh got up there just as those two miners straining ahead on their clumsy draft animals, came running through.

The other miners roared in relief as those two burst into sight, swung their animals half around, sprang down and raced back to join the others. Their rawboned leader checked his rifle, stepped boldly into the pass, threw up his gun and fired. A thousand yards ahead a big, wicked-horned steer lost his footing and went down. The other miners sprang into action firing head-on into the first rank of those charging cattle, dropping steers and cows end over end. Whether it was the pile-up of dead animals or the face-on crimson flash of all those exploding guns Hugh never knew, but at the last possible moment his cattle broke, some swinging left, some whirling right. Behind them other hundreds of blind-running half-ton beasts followed the leaders until, ten minutes later, the pass was chokingly filled with coarse dust, but no cattle tried coming through.

The ground was still shaking when Hugh swung down and walked up where that old leathery-faced miner was calmly reloading his long-barrelled Springfield.

'I didn't think you boys could turn them,' he said, watching that rough-tough older man reload. 'I'm obliged to you. If they'd busted out through this pass they'd have run out as far as the Fort Collins road, and after that . . .' Hugh lifted his shoulders and dropped them.

The rawboned older man fixed Hugh with a steady eye. 'Easier'n breakin' a buffler stampede,' he laconically said. 'Your critters, mister?'

'They're mine, yes.'

'Well now, if you'd be willin' to sell us them dead ones yonder we'd sure be much obliged.' The older man cracked his lips in a smile. 'Y'see, we been livin' on salt pork 'cause every damned town we hit so far, this late in the rush, has been plumb out'n fresh meat.'

Hugh admired this Southerner's complete confidence and calmness. He smiled back. 'Help yourself and feel welcome. If it hadn't been for you I'd have probably lost the whole herd.'

'Obliged,' said the rawboned man, nodding. 'Much obliged, stranger. What you reckon started that danged stampede anyway?'

Hugh turned, sprang back into the saddle and gathered his reins up short. 'I don't know but I've got a suspicion,' he said, and moved on past up through the dust-choked pass again. 'Good luck at the diggings,' he sang out, and the miners waved their hats at him.

For a mile on into this valley Hugh couldn't see more than a hundred feet ahead. The dust hung high overhead. It had a rank smell and a salty taste. His mount repeatedly cleared its nostrils. It was this constant snorting that eventually brought forth through the pall of dust a croaked order for Hugh to halt right where he was or take the consequences.

He halted, but he also recognised that waspish voice. 'Stumpy,' he called out, 'what're you doin' way out here?'

134

The *cosinero* came limping through the tan murk to halt and peer and say something harsh under his breath as he grounded his Winchester, drew up one leg and gingerly massaged the ankle.

'Well, I can tell you one thing,' exclaimed Stumpy. 'I sure-'nough didn't *fly* out here.'

Hugh got down, walked over and said, 'What happened?'

'I dunno exactly,' answered Stumpy, lowering his injured leg very carefully and testing it with his whole weight. He swore with enormous relief and almost smiled. 'Lordy, figured it was broke sure. I was scootin' along and somehow a consarned steer got under m'horse; gutted him and spilt us both. Hurt my blasted ankle when I rolled on it—or something.' Stumpy suddenly changed expression, looked around and said, 'We 'uns as was at the wagon never had a chance, Hugh, an' if the ground hadn't been hard as rock so's we could feel the tremblin' underfoot, we'd have got ground to mincemeat.'

'What started it?'

'I don't know. One minute I was fixin' dinner an' the next minute Tex flashed past screechin' like a Comanche for us to get astride, that it was a stampede. Then there was some shootin' out where I think Cowan and Milt were ridin'.' Stumpy stopped speaking, turned completely around and gazed far off where two dust-banners were flashing skyward under the encouragement of those racing cattle.

Hugh brought his horse in closer. 'Get in the saddle,' he ordered. 'Here, give me your carbine until you're mounted.' After Stumpy got astride Hugh sprang up behind him. As they headed for the camp Hugh watched those two dust-banners eventually come together over near the foothills below Fortier Pass, and after that the run-out cattle slowed gradually until they were no longer raising any dust at all.

The wagon was miraculously upright and untouched but their texas was completely destroyed as was the rope-corral. Stumpy looked at his trampled pans, upset coffee pot, ruined stone-ring, and swore with deep feeling.

Hugh dismounted, stepped over the wreckage and went over by the wagon's right side to look far out where two horsemen were coming towards him in a loose lope. Stumpy was mutteringly hobbling around salvaging things, his imprecations, while addressed to no one in particular, nonetheless blistering for all that.

The pair of riders were Cowan and Tex Rathbone. The moment they spotted Hugh they hurried on in, swung down and Cowan said, 'No accident, Hugh. They hit the herd from over by the foothills. Hit it on the run shootin' over the cattle.'

Rathbone stepped past, looped his reins and

climbed up to grope inside the wagon. When he stepped back down again he had a box of carbine bullets in one hand. Hugh watched him walk over and drop the shells into his saddlebag without a word, loosen his reins and turn to mount up.

Hugh said, 'Hold it, Tex. Where d'you think you're going?'

Rathbone mounted and looked downward. 'After a murderer, Hugh. Milt's dead out there.'

Stumpy heard that and drew up to his full height staring over at the Texan. Hugh and Cowan exchanged a look. Cowan solemnly inclined his head.

'The kid got trampled, Hugh. He was in front an' couldn't get clear. Him an' his horse both.'

Tex straightened up and lifted his reins. Hugh said, 'Hold it; you're not going anywhere.'

The lanky Texan looked down his nose. 'No?' he drawled, still with his rein-hand up and ready to spin his horse.

'No! First we bring Milt in. Next we bury him.'

'And after that?' asked the Texan softly.

Hugh said, 'After that—yes. We'll find Ed Morrow and ask some questions.'

Rathbone slowly dropped his left hand and inclined his head. 'We'll need a blanket,' he said. 'Milt's in a bad way.'

They all turned towards the south as a new sound of shod hooves striking hard upon flinty soil came to them. Johnny Emerson loped up white in the face and hatless. He was badly shaken. As he slowed and eventually halted he looked at the others from troubled eyes, spat dust, and said, 'That was close. If I hadn't had a real good animal under me I'd never have made it.'

'Get caught in front?' asked Cowan tonelessly, and when Johnny nodded Cowan said in the same cornhusk dry, inflectionless way, 'So did Milt. Only he wasn't so lucky.' He looked over at Stumpy. 'Fetch us a blanket or a big piece of canvas an' while we're gone, Stumpy, hunt up the shovel and get to digging.'

Emerson's face changed completely. He and Milt Stillwell had been riding pardners right from the start over in Idaho. 'Milt . . . ?' he whispered.

Cowan nodded. 'Couldn't get clear, Johnny. They went over him an' his horse, maybe a thousand head of 'em.'

Emerson slumped.

Hugh stepped over beside Tex Rathbone's bent knee and looked up into the saturnine Texan's bronzed, lean face. 'What did you see out there after the gunfire started?'

'Three horsemen. Two ridin' bays, one ridin' a flashy chestnut horse with a flaxen mane and tail, Hugh. They had to be waitin' in the foothills. Art and I discussed that on the way back. If they were waitin' in the rocks, then they had to be waitin' for you to ride off with Marshal Coleman.'

Hugh stepped back and no one could have told from the look of him that Hugh Benedict had ever known how to smile.

Stumpy brought them out a torn and trampled piece of their canvas from the texas. Cowan took this, rolled it up and got back astride. Johnny Emerson moved out his horse as Rathbone and Cowan turned, but Hugh halted him with an order.

'Go find the horses, Johnny. Fetch 'em back. Stumpy and I'll set the corral up again.' Johnny looked ready to protest so Hugh shook his head at him. 'Do like I tell you and take my word for it—you don't want to see Milt right now. Now go run in the horses.'

Cowan and Rathbone, riding off, half-turned in their saddles, both gravely nodded over at Emerson, then straightened back around as they moved off under that dusty, mustard-tan evil overhead sun.

Emerson finally turned and walked his animal out the way he'd just entered camp. Hugh and Stumpy watched him for a moment before Stumpy sniffled, ran a shirtsleeve under his nose and limped resolutely out where the rope-corral was scattered over five acres of churned, soiled earth.

Hugh had nothing to say and neither did the *cosinero*. They had to splice their corral ropes in six places but they had the corral reassembled a good half-hour before they saw Emerson returning with their loose-stock, and for once neither the freed animals or the cowboy hazing them into camp, were moving any faster than a wilted walk.

It was not hard to corral the horses. They were as run-out as the cattle also were. Their hides glistened with sweat and their lung-cages still heaved from the wild race.

Stumpy did what he could towards making the camp presentable and he said not one word all the time he hobbled around on his fearfully swollen ankle doing all this, which was in its own way grimly significant.

Hugh and Johnny took the shovel out a way and worked in relays digging Milt's grave. Sweat rolled off them in rivulets but neither had a word to say until Johnny, resting while Hugh dug, spotted Cowan and Rathbone returning with that evil-shrouded sun falling away behind them.

'It was the Fortier outfit, wasn't it, Hugh?'

'I reckon, Johnny. But we need proof.'

'Yeah. Well, we'll get it. But why Milt?'

Hugh didn't answer. He'd seen men trampled to death in other stampedes. He'd also heard that same question asked before too. He threw off sweat and continued to square up the deep, long hole, halting only when Cowan and Rathbone grimly halted ten feet away and dismounted with their claret-stained filthy piece of laden canvas.

## CHAPTER FOURTEEN

They stood bareheaded while Hugh read from
the Book over Milt Stillwell's lumpy grave.
Sweat rolled off them. They were shaken and
filthy and red-eyed from abrasive dust. Johnny
Emerson's tanned face was white and his eyes
had an unnatural glaze to them. When the
others finished paying their last respects and
walked quietly back to the wagon Johnny
remained behind. He and Milt had been close.

Stumpy had coffee brewed but no one
accepted the cups he offered and Tex
Rathbone took out his long-bladed knife and
picked up a piece of wood to begin whittling.
Tex was thinking. After a while, as Hugh
returned with Art Cowan from an inspection
of the rope-corral and the horses, he said
without looking up or missing a stroke with
that wicked-bladed big knife: 'Any of the
horses skinned up?'

'No,' said Cowan. 'They're all right. Just a
couple of bruises. But we're short a few head.'

'At least two,' stated Hugh, dropping down
beside Stumpy's little fire, not because he was
thirsty or hungry but purely out of long habit.
'Stumpy had one gored under him.'

Tex lifted his head, looked through the

141

murky, hushed atmosphere and snapped his knife closed. 'Rider comin',' he said quietly, and kept watching the eastward plain until he could satisfy himself about something. Then he dourly grunted. 'That damned lawman again.'

Hugh met Coleman and saw in the marshal's expression that he'd either been told by those goldminers out near the yonder pass something had happened, or else he'd read all the sign as he'd ridden on in.

But there was one thing Coleman wouldn't know so Hugh bluntly said, 'Milt got trampled to death, Jack.'

Coleman took this without flinching, but his pale eyes turned dry and hard. 'What caused it?' he asked.

'Three riders shooting over the herd and charging into it.'

'You see 'em, Hugh?'

'He didn't,' spoke up Tex. 'But I did. Two ridin' bays and one on a flashy chestnut with a light mane an' tail.'

'You didn't see the riders?'

Tex made a wry face but he also wagged his head. 'There wasn't a whole lot o' time once they commenced firin' guns, Marshal. All the same we know who it was.'

Coleman looked at Hugh again. 'Milt,' he murmured. 'That was the young, straw-haired feller with the boyish grin.'

Stumpy said, 'You want some coffee,' and

didn't make a question of it at all, made it sound instead as though he was asking whether Coleman wanted to be hated or not.

'No, thanks.' Coleman turned, gazed northward through the mustard-tan atmosphere and said softly, 'Who's that standin' out yonder?'

'That's Johnny Emerson,' said Hugh. 'We buried Milt out there. Johnny and Milt were pretty close.'

'Pardners,' stated Tex, back at his whittling again. 'You ever lose a pardner like this, Marshal?'

Hugh turned and silenced Tex with a look. Cowan walked over, took one of Stumpy's filled cups and sipped the hot beverage while staring up towards Fortier Pass.

'You got it figured out why he'd do anything as pointless as this?' Coleman asked Benedict.

Hugh said, 'I think so. First off, he got you away from here. It wasn't getting me out of the valley he was worrying about, like we thought. It was using me to get *you* out, Marshal. You and your posse. After that, he headed that stampede straight for the pass and out there towards the Fort Collins road. If these critters had got down onto that road they'd have raised hell and also, they'd have kept on running until they were scattered from here to Kingdom Come.'

'Take you maybe a week or two to gather them up again, Hugh?'

'Yeah. At least that long. And it's a safe bet I never would recover at least half of them.'

Coleman put down his empty cup and said quietly, 'I'm beginning to make sense out of this.'

'Kind of late though, ain't it?' muttered Stumpy, sitting on the wagon tailgate with his boot off and his purpling, badly sprained ankle exposed. 'Sort of like lockin' the barn after the horse's been stolen.'

Coleman gazed over at Stumpy. He also considered wintry-eyed Tex Rathbone and Art Cowan. 'One of the interestin' things about life,' he said mildly to those three, 'is that if we could see into the future the past sure would be different an' the present would be so blamed peaceful and dull we'd all die of boredom.' He paused, but none of those three had any comment to make, so he said, 'I need some deputies for what's ahead, boys.'

Johnny Emerson came walking up in time to hear this. He put a bitter look at Marshal Coleman. 'You do whatever you got to do, your way,' he said. 'I'll do what I got to do my way.'

Tex closed his knife with that audible snapping sound again but this time he pocketed the thing. He was looking from Hugh to Coleman and on over to Emerson. Tex not only had the eyesight of an eagle, he also had a feeling for impending trouble. He had that feeling now.

144

Hugh, also eyeing Emerson, said, 'Easy, Johnny. The marshal's going to square things for Milt.'

'Is he? How; by standin' around here askin' a lot of damfool questions? I know a better way.'

Emerson started walking on past heading out for his horse. Hugh let him get part of the way past before he called to him.

'Johnny, you ride with the rest of us, not alone. You head across this valley right now an' they'll have you in their sights before you're half-way to the foothills.'

'Let 'em,' tossed back Emerson, and kept right on walking.

'Johnny, the odds are five-to-one. You'd never get close enough for one shot.'

Emerson spun back around. He had his .45 out and aimed. His face was bitter. 'We've sat around near a week waitin' for some damned female to play square. All we've done by waitin' is get Milt killed an' lose most of the lead we had on those other herds behind us. Sorry, Hugh, but I like my way better'n yours.'

Tex said quietly, 'Put up the gun, Johnny. Hugh's right. We'll square things with Morrow for Milt, only we got to do it legal-like.'

Emerson shifted to include Rathbone, Cowan and even old Stumpy, in the radius of his levelled gun. 'Legal-like, Tex? That don't mean killin' Morrow for what he did here today. That only means haulin' him into court

145

an' gettin' him maybe two, three years in prison. Well, I want more'n that for Milt, an' I'm goin' to get it.'

Tex said: 'Johnny! You figure to kill me too?'

Emerson's bitter eyes wavered. 'What you mean?' he demanded.

'I'm goin' to draw on you, Johnny. Damned if I'm goin' to let you ride out of here like this an' get yourself killed. If you did that there'd only be me'n Art and Hugh left to buck Morrow and his five guns. Even with the marshal I don't think we'd stand too good a chance against 'em. We need your gun too, but on the side of the law now. Not like you're figurin' on doing. So you put up that gun—or you use it—one or the other.'

Emerson stood out there staring hard at the Texan trying to satisfy himself whether Rathbone would really draw on him or not. It was a bad moment for all of them. Hugh almost spoke, but checked himself. Whatever decision embittered Johnny Emerson came to now, he'd have to arrive at it all by himself.

'You wouldn't,' he finally whispered, and Tex said right back, 'I'd have to, Johnny. I wouldn't want to so help me—but I'd *have* to. That's the only way we got any chance against the Fortier outfit at all. All of us together. Each one backin' up the others.'

Emerson's gun-muzzle sagged. Art Cowan let out a quiet sigh and loosened where he

146

stood. Stumpy swallowed, cleared his throat and garrulously said, 'Well, don't just stand around. Someone go rig out the horses an' someone else fetch my buffler rifle out'n the wagon. And Johnny, how about helpin' me get this damned boot back on.'

Marshal Coleman, acting as though they hadn't all just lived through a bad moment, looked at Stumpy's badly swollen ankle and shook his head. 'Better just wrap it in cloth,' he quietly said. 'You'll never get that boot back on it.'

Hugh jerked his head at Cowan. Those two started on out towards the rope-corral. They passed Johnny Emerson without a look or a word.

They left the wagon-camp with the sun slanting away towards the west, Johnny and Tex riding together, Art Cowan and Stumpy Crawford side by side, and up front out in the lead, Jack Coleman and Hugh Benedict. They passed near the spot where Milt Stillwell's trampled horse lay and except for Marshal Coleman's long look in that direction the others glanced out then looked quickly away again.

There wasn't much conversation after that until they hit the foothills. By then the sun was reddening and the land lay soft-hazed as much from particles of dust in the atmosphere as from late-day heat-haze.

Where Coleman halted them they shared a

common conviction. Ed Morrow would have a watcher up the pass somewhere, perhaps near the top-out, but wherever that man was, by now he'd have seen them coming and would probably have signalled down into Fortier Valley.

'Two ways to skin a cat,' said Coleman as he gazed out of squinted eyes up near the top-out. 'One is to take out your knife an' go to work. The other way is to keep puttin' it off until you're driven to it. I've always liked the first way best, but maybe goin' over into that damned valley this time of day isn't very wise.'

'Morrow'll be waiting,' opined Tex Rathbone. 'Pretty hard to do much good in the dark in a place where your enemy knows the ground and you don't.'

'Exactly,' said Coleman, and glanced around at the others but particularly at stocky Johnny Emerson.

Hugh finished a quiet inspection of the roundabout hilltops and said, 'Something else occurs to me, boys. By now we've been seen coming up here. They'll know our destination and they'll be out there somewhere, waiting. But suppose Ed Morrow who knows all the trail hereabouts decided to let us drift past in the dark?'

'What of it?' asked Emerson, eyeing Hugh sulphurously. 'We could still hunt him down.'

'I'm not worrying about finding Morrow,' Hugh replied. 'What I'm wondering about is simply this—he wants to bust up our drive badly enough to get one of us killed for it, so what's to stop him from passing around us in the dark with his crew, getting back down there and *really* stampeding the cattle this time—while we're up in Fortier Valley?'

This thought held them all silent for a long time. Eventually Cowan gravely nodded. So did Tex and Stumpy. Johnny sat grimly unmoving for a while, then he too nodded, but he added a new fear to this by saying, 'You're right, Hugh, and if there's a bunch of miners camped outside our valley alongside the road out there, them cattle might trample a whole lot more folks too.'

Marshal Coleman lifted his reins, turned his horse off the main trail and rolled his head at them. 'Come along then,' he ordered. 'I know a pretty good spot to bed down.'

None of them had bedrolls with them but this wasn't any particular inconvenience because they all had their coats tied aft of the cantle and they also had their saddle-blankets, things men of their kind had improvised into temporary beds more than once over the years.

Food, which might have ordinarily been a factor, was not now. All but a couple of them had recently looked upon what remained of a friend after a thousand head of cattle had gone over him. Food was far from their thoughts right then.

Coleman angled around through the broken

country with what seemed to Hugh Benedict to be experienced sagacity because he always managed to have a peak or a rim or a hillside between them and the higher-up road up Fortier Pass. It was no accident, of course, but the way Coleman slouched along it almost seemed like one, that he consistently kept them shielded from surprise attack as well as from that upwards viewing.

Where he finally halted, with dusk sootily settling, there was a little creek that boiled out of solid rock, ran southward a hundred yards and disappeared into a pit of bottomless sand. There was good grass here and myriad animal tracks. There were also several shaggy old trees and a flourishing stand of buckbrush.

They removed the bridles but not the saddles from their horses and let the animals wander off to graze. Stumpy went downstream and bathed his swollen ankle in water so cold it made him gasp. The others cleared a little space and made up their makeshift beds. Art Cowan dropped down near Emerson, offered his tobacco sack and these two were more or less thoughtfully silent. Tex disappeared northward with his carbine in hand, on a little scouting expedition, while Jack Coleman and Hugh Benedict came together near the game-trail they'd used to reach this spot, and squatted over there where they could keep an eye on the horses.

'Morrow'll hear about us comin' up into the

foothills,' said Marshal Coleman. 'He'll have a spy or two atop the hills to pass the word back to him.'

'Unless he's already slipped by and is heading for my herd again,' said Hugh.

'I doubt that. At least for now I figure he'll be both curious and worried about what we're up to. He'll want to make plumb sure about us before he tries hitting your herd again.' Coleman pushed back his hat and looked over where the others were dark-blending silhouettes in the deepening dusk. 'Besides,' he went on, 'he saw what he'll think is your whole crew ride up into these hills. He won't know yet that I'm with you in the place of one of your men. He won't know yet, Hugh, that he killed a man today, and I'm countin' pretty heavily on that, because if he knew I wanted to talk to him about a murder, I think we'd be seein' an entirely different Ed Morrow.'

Hugh said no more for a long while; he squatted there listening to the night, gauging its silence, testing its atmosphere, swinging his head from left to right and back again. He doubted that Morrow would attack them, but he also thought this was not entirely impossible; thought that if by some chance Morrow *did* know he'd murdered a man today, that he would then, as Jack Coleman had intimated, fling caution to the wind because a man can't be hung any higher for six murders than he can for one.

# CHAPTER FIFTEEN

Rathbone came back as silently as he'd departed but he had nothing to report. 'Too blamed dark,' he growled. 'You get a hundred yards away from this place an' you can't hardly find your hat with both hands, let alone find your way back. But I didn't hear or smell anything. No tobacco smoke, no horse sweat.'

Coleman listened and quietly said, 'But they'll likely be out there doin' a little scoutin' of their own.' He looked over where Hugh was standing, gazing around into the stygian night.

Hugh came closer to those two and said, 'Suppose we start out right now? By leading our horses and taking plenty of time we could use every bit of this full darkness, before the moon comes up and gives us away.'

Rathbone liked the idea and said so, but Marshal Coleman had one reservation. 'Your *cosinero* couldn't walk a hundred feet on that sprained leg of his.'

Tex had the answer to that. 'Let him ride. I'll lead his horse and mine too.'

Hugh said, 'Go tell the others, Tex, and tell them to make no noise when they catch their animals. Jack and I'll wait up here for the lot of you.'

Rathbone had been gone only a few moments when Hugh said softly, 'Jack, losing

Milt wasn't all of it. Losing faith in Meredith Fortier hurt just as much.'

Coleman stood silently nodding. 'I'm in my fifties, Hugh, and down the years I've consistently looked for integrity in people. Sometimes I've found it but not too often, an' that sort of knocks the illusions out of a man after a while. But somehow a man always looks up to a handsome woman; sort of feels like he's breathing a particularly clean breath of air when he's around one.' Coleman sighed. 'I know exactly how you feel. I knew she'd be tough. I guess I even knew she'd fight you although I didn't want to believe that. But when she refused to even come out of the house the other night when I rode in up there, and she had an armed cowboy on her porch to keep me from pushin' my way in without a warrant, that pretty well destroyed the last of my illusions.'

The men came walking quietly. Cowan had told them to remove their spurs, which they'd done, and he had made another change. Instead of Rathbone leading two horses, one with crippled Stumpy aboard, Cowan was leading Stumpy along and Johnny Emerson had Tex's animal. Cowan explained this change to Hugh when he walked on up.

'Tex is the best scout we got. Let him go ahead and pick the way for us.'

Hugh and Marshal Coleman agreed with this, Rathbone glided on ahead into the formless night, and with Hugh leading out they left their little creekside meadow winding northward through the broken country.

They walked along in Rathbone's shadow for a full hour before briefly halting. Tex said the land was steeper on ahead, that he couldn't find a pass around or through the onward hills so they would have to climb. They climbed; it wasn't easy and once, when Art Cowan fell and afterwards cursed, they rested for a while. Coleman told Hugh they were passing up around the south slope of Fortier Pass, but well away from the main trail.

It was near midnight before Tex trotted back to say he'd skylined the onward slope and they were near its crest. Hugh told Rathbone to cut lower down, not to lead them across that skyline, and Tex dutifully obeyed.

It was gruelling work but none of them complained. When they frequently paused to 'blow' their horses though, the men were relieved to be able to rest also.

The last time on the south slope that Tex came back he pointed up where the far-away higher mountains stood dark-hulking against a pewter sky. 'The moon's coming,' he said. 'We got to be over the hump before it lights things up or they'll spot us sure.'

For a steady half hour the men dragged their animals and pushed themselves, but they got around the south slope and began angling downward at once, making good time now upon this open hillside, driven to their greatest and final effort by fear of moonlight.

Ultimately, as the lopsided old moon lifted serenely above its distant ramparts, they got down into Fortier Valley. When Tex came back to report no sound anywhere around, no movement, Hugh pointed over towards the westward fringe of forest and hiked on. Until they got into the speckled gloom of those giant trees they were exposed, but afterwards they were quite safe.

Cowan dropped down. So did Marshal Coleman and Johnny Emerson. Stumpy eased down off his saddle and hopped upon his one good leg until he was also upon that spongy, fragrant carpeting of pine needles, then he too went down. Hugh alone remained standing. While the others lay panting Hugh and Tex angled off on foot around through the forest-fringe for a glimpse of the distant ranch buildings.

When they finally could make them out under the pale glow of that crooked old moon, Tex said one word: 'Dark.'

There was no light anywhere out where the buildings stood. In fact, the way they were situated in a rough circle, they appeared as forted-up wagons rather than ranch buildings. Rathbone commented on this where he stood with Hugh in among the trees.

'Be pretty hard to sneak up on that place the way someone planned them buildings—if there's a sentry down there.'

There was only one way to find out if there was a sentry but Hugh didn't mention it. His solemn gaze towards Meredith's main house was quietly hostile. 'There may be a man watching,' he said to Tex, 'but he's not important. Neither is the girl. What we want is Morrow, and if he's not at the bunkhouse, which I doubt like the devil, then he'll be somewhere up near the pass, maybe, or somewhere around us in the night, because he knows by now we were coming this way before sundown.'

Rathbone thought a moment, rolled his brows together and said, 'Then why all the rush to get up here, Hugh? Why didn't we just wait until dawn an' go huntin' him?'

'Because, come dawn, I figure, if Morrow isn't at the bunkhouse, we *will* be. He'll show up here sooner or later. When he does I'd like to surprise him; take him without a fight if possible.'

Tex ran a dirty hand over his whiskery chin making a small grating sound in the quiet. He nodded, raised his head and looked out at those buildings again. 'Sounds reasonable,' he commented. 'Well, reckon we'd better go back and get the others.'

They returned the way they had come. The moon was making its belated crossing through a field of pure white stars. The night was turning chilly and its piled-up silence was

156

endless.

Marshal Coleman had put on his coat by the time Tex and Hugh got back. So had Stumpy, and he was also massaging his swollen, blanket-wrapped injured ankle. There was a constant look of anguish in his hat-shadowed eyes but Stumpy was the kind of man who would die before he would complain. He was also the kind of a man who would suffer stoically for as long as he had to, in order to be where he wanted to be with a gun when someone he viewed as an unregenerate enemy would appear.

Johnny Emerson and Art Cowan were standing together near their rested horses but when Hugh appeared Cowan strode over to him.

'Heard a horse a while back,' he said softly, and pointed back the way they had come. He dropped his arm. 'It could've been a loose animal and it could've been a ridden one. It didn't make enough steady noise for any of us to be sure.'

Hugh jerked his head at Tex. 'Go back a ways and look around,' he ordered. 'I doubt if they could know we came this way but we can't afford to underestimate anyone either.'

Tex dutifully moved off. Coleman walked up, watched Rathbone disappear, and asked about the buildings. Hugh told him they were quiet, dark, and seemingly unguarded. Coleman thought about this for a while, still gazing southward the way Tex had faded out.

'But they won't be unguarded,' he finally said, sounding quietly confident about this. 'You know, even after the Indians no longer raided down here old Jules always had his men stand night-watch at the ranch just like he always had them ride night-herd. It was a strong habit.' Coleman swung his eyes to Hugh. 'Ed Morrow is of the same old-time school. He'll fight exactly the same way.'

'We can find his sentry, take care of him, and get inside the bunkhouse, Jack. Then we can out-wait Morrow. Sooner or later he's going to return to the ranch.'

'All right,' agreed the shrewd, imperturbable lawman. 'But let's do this like Morrow and the Indians would do it. Let's stay on these pine needles where we'll leave no tracks.'

Tex returned a half-hour later when they were all rested and getting impatient again. He said he hadn't found either loose horses or riders.

They boosted old Stumpy back into his saddle and started on towards the Fortier Ranch buildings with indefatigable Tex Rathbone in the lead again. They made no noise and they went slowly and cautiously. Hugh was confident that if Morrow had left a man at the ranch, he'd also left this man with orders to signal, probably with gunshots, if anything untoward occurred.

Marshal Coleman walked beside his horse

with his Winchester cradled in one arm. He was the oldest man among them but he seemed as revived and alert as any of the younger ones.

Rathbone halted where the trees formed a protruding wedge down upon the grassy plain. This was the same spot Hugh had hidden his horse in twice now. It was also the same spot where Art Cowan had left his mount the night he'd slipped up behind that cowboy who had thrown-down on Hugh. It was less than a hundred yards from the yonder buildings and there was no more suitable place close by for their purpose, so Johnny Emerson helped Stumpy to dismount, they all tied their horses in filigreed shadows, and stood grouped up close studying the onward buildings.

Johnny Emerson had his carbine in both hands up across his body. He said in a strong whisper to Hugh, 'Let me go down there. I'll find him.'

'Yeah,' whispered Art Cowan dryly, 'but it'd be better if we didn't scalp any of 'em unnecessarily.'

Emerson turned to darkly frown at Art. Hugh touched Tex's sleeve asking: 'You up to it? You've done about twice the foot-work as the rest of us.'

Rathbone's long lip lifted to disclose white teeth. 'I'm up to it,' he said, and handed Marshal Coleman his carbine. 'Won't need this,' he said, and moved away from them

159

northward through the trees. They lost sight of him almost at once.

The wait was a long one. Johnny muttered something under his breath after twenty minutes had gone by. Stumpy too, became both anxious for Tex and impatient about the delay. Cowan, Hugh, Marshal Coleman, stood like statues straining to hear sounds or sight movements. They picked up neither. The moon continued on its right-to-left crossing, the endless hush ran on, those sinister-looking buildings out there circled up fort-like as they were, seemed to be some kind of a trap in the night. Eventually Hugh caught some of the contagious uneasiness around him and gauged the amount of time which had passed from the moon's passing.

He was considering going ahead himself to find Tex, to determine what had gone wrong, when Stumpy gave a little gasp and a little start where he stood, swinging his carbine as he twisted around. It was Tex. He'd returned even more quietly than he'd departed. He wickedly grinned at old Stumpy, put out a long arm, tipped the *cosinero*'s aimed gunbarrel away from his chest and stepped on past.

'He was at the house on the front porch where I sort of figured he just might be,' Tex related as the others crowded close to hear each whispered word. 'I laid him out colder'n a block of ice an' you know something, he already had a danged goose-egg on his head

160

where someone else had hit him before.'

'Any others?' Hugh asked, ignoring Tex's triumphant broad grin.

'None that I could find, and I pretty well scouted-up the whole blessed place. That's why I been gone so long.'

'The bunkhouse?' asked Marshal Coleman.

'Empty as a last year's bird nest, Marshal. So's the barn, the shoein' shed, even the hen-house.' Tex let his grin die. 'I didn't look around the main-house very much; figured that woman'd be in there and if she had a gun an' heard me it might not be too good for the lot of us.'

Hugh silenced the others with a word, then gestured onward. 'Take us out and around, Tex; take us the best way to the bunkhouse.'

They had a problem. Stumpy, even using his carbine as a crutch, couldn't hobble very fast so they had to slow their own progress to his best efforts. If this annoyed any of them they didn't let it show, and meanwhile Stumpy did the best he could with Johnny Emerson, who was also short, to give him a shoulder now and then.

Rathbone coursed ahead, returned and coursed ahead again. He seemed to be immensely enjoying himself at this silent, stalking business. One moment his lanky, lean frame was there before them in the trees, the next moment it had disappeared. But he took them around behind the silent buildings, down

161

through the forest where it came closest to Fortier Ranch's network of working corrals, and with an absolute minimum of exposure he led them unerringly straight up behind the deserted bunkhouse.

They got inside one at a time, then Hugh and Tex went back after the sentry Rathbone had knocked out. They dragged and carried this man into the bunkhouse with them, gagged and bound him, and finally, with the small hours of this long, fraught night growing larger as dawn came constantly closer, they were where both Hugh and Marshal Coleman had wanted them to be before daylight arrived again.

'If they just ride on in,' muttered Cowan fervently, 'and don't go pokin' up there where we left the horses, I reckon we'll have this thing wrapped up without firin' a shot within another few hours.'

Johnny Emerson agreed with this, but he didn't sound pleased at the prospect. 'The law'll never in God's green world hang Morrow for Milt,' he said bitterly. 'The law'll hold he wasn't directly responsible for Milt bein' in front of them damned cattle. I've seen the law work before.'

Marshal Coleman gazed at Johnny but he didn't argue; he didn't say anything to anyone in fact, he simply drew out his six-gun, spun the cylinder to check the loads, then quietly returned the gun to its holster.

# CHAPTER SIXTEEN

Time passed on leaden feet. The cowboy Tex had knocked out moaned, weakly struggled against his bonds and opened his eyes to bewilderedly look around. What he saw gave him a brief relapse; he either fainted or simply dropped back into unconsciousness again from being struck over the head, but in either case he slumped and Stumpy, bending over him, made a disgusted little clucking sound deep in his throat.

'In my day it took a sight more'n a whack over the skull to keep a good man down.'

'He isn't a good man,' growled Johnny, and this effectively silenced Stumpy.

Tex slouched over beside the opened doorway with Cowan and Marshal Coleman. When Hugh came forward Coleman said, 'I've been turning over in my mind the chances of slippin' into the house and taking Meredith prisoner. Holding her here with us as a hostage.'

Hugh shook his head. 'Suppose a couple of us got caught over there when Morrow returns. Or suppose she awakened and fired a shot.'

Tex smiled at Coleman, his narrowed eyes calculating. 'You kind of like this notion of hostages, don't you?' he asked.

Coleman looked at Rathbone, matched Tex's grin and said, 'I forgot to tell you boys something when I was explainin' how old Jules and Ed Morrow fight like the Indians used to fight, I learnt in the same school. Hostages were a big part of any campaign. It was a good system; it usually worked.'

'And when it didn't?' asked Tex.

Coleman shrugged, lost his grin, and turned to gaze out across the moonlighted silent yard. 'Well then—sometimes the hostages didn't fare so well,' he said.

Hugh was impatient. Twice he asked Cowan what time it was. He still thought it quite likely that Morrow would hit his herd again. If he did, if the cattle found that pass out of the valley in the dark, he would lose everything anyway.

Stumpy made his little chirping sound. The captive was coming around again. All of them except Tex Rathbone left the doorway and went over to drop down and hear what this man had to say. At first he was only concerned with a headache which he described graphically and unprintably as being the grand-daddy of all headaches. Then he asked Stumpy to fetch him a bottle of whisky which he said was in a warbag hanging from the foot of a bunk he indicated.

Stumpy astonished all his companions by jumping up on his one good leg, hopping unerringly to that cowboy's warbag, digging out the bottle and hopping straight back again.

'You damned fraud,' said Johnny Emerson to the *cosinero*. 'An' all the time I thought you was sufferin' the pains of the damned.'

Stumpy gravely winked at Emerson. When the Fortier rider reached for his bottle though, old Stumpy jerked it away. He worked out the cork, tilted his head and took two long pulls before lowering the bottle and rapidly blinking as he offered the whisky around. No one took any so Stumpy finally, almost reluctantly, handed it to the cowboy. They waited for that liquor to do its work. When it did Hugh said, 'What's your name?' to the Fortier rider.

'Wesley. They call me Wes.'

'Wes, where's Ed Morrow?'

Wes shook his head, stopped doing this suddenly and put both hands to his temples. 'I don't know. Him an' the others left before sundown. Ed told me to keep watch an' if any of you showed up to fire two rounds, count ten, then fire another two rounds.'

'Where was he going when he left here?'

Wes shrugged. 'He didn't say, but I figured he was goin' to hit your herd again. Either that or bushwhack the lot of you.'

Marshal Coleman, up until now in the background, eased around Hugh's shoulder and said, 'Me too, cowboy?'

Wes looked, dropped his eyes from that shadowed face to the dull glint on Coleman's shirtfront, and looked swiftly up again. 'Hell,' he gasped. 'How come you to be here, Marshal; we figured you was down in Denver.'

'Well, I'll tell you how come,' said Coleman softly. 'Whenever there's a murder I get mighty interested.'

'Murder . . .?' whispered Wes, his face turning tight and pale. 'Who got murdered?'

'That stampede today, cowboy, went over one of Mister Benedict's riders. He died under about a thousand head of stampedin' cattle.'

Wes's mouth dropped. His round eyes lingered in a stricken way upon Marshal Coleman.

Johnny Emerson put forth a hand to lightly tap Wes on the shoulder and get his attention. Then Johnny said, 'What colour horse you been ridin' lately, Wes?'

The cowboy looked around at Johnny. 'Black colt,' he said, 'with two white stockings in front. Why? You tryin' to fit me into that stampede?' Wes shook his head and this time he ignored the little hammers inside his skull such a motion set to pounding. 'No you don't,' he told Johnny Emerson. 'I been right here on the ranch all day by Ed's orders.'

'Sentry?' asked Marshal Coleman, and the cowboy said something that startled them all.

'Call it sentry if you like. I call it more like bein' a jailer.'

Hugh and Jack Coleman both strained forward at the same time. 'Whose jailer?' asked Hugh swiftly. 'Speak up, man: whose

166

jailer?'

'Hers,' rapped out Wes.

For a long moment no one said anything. Hugh stood up and gazed thoughtfully downwards. Marshal Coleman also stood up, but he let off a rattling long breath and half turned away. After a little time he said, 'Well, some of my faith in humanity is restored. Some of it.' He faced their captive once more. 'Explain,' he ordered. 'Speak up, cowboy.'

'Well, there ain't much to explain, Marshal. After this Benedict feller snuck in here two nights together without us knowin' it, Ed said we'd have to keep him out of Fortier Valley some other way. That last time he snuck in Miss Meredith and Ed had an argument. First one they ever had, some of the older riders said, but I can tell you one thing—it was a lulu. We could hear 'em all the way over to the bunkhouse. And Marshal—the night you rode in an' asked to see her—well—that's the night Ed put me to guardin' her with orders to shoot anyone, you included, who tried to talk to her. It sort of struck me that I wasn't so much her guard as her jailer. That's what I meant a minute ago when I said I was more jailer'n guard.'

'What was that argument about?' asked Hugh. 'You said you could hear 'em as far off as this bunkhouse. What were they yelling about?'

'You, mostly. You an' your cattle comin'

through Fortier Valley.'

'What about it?'

But Wes couldn't give any better answer because he hadn't been able to piece the words into any sensible sequence. 'I'll sure tell you one thing though,' he said. 'Ed was madder'n I've ever seen him since hirin' out to Fortier Ranch, when he got back to the bunkhouse.'

Hugh brushed his fingers over Jack Coleman's forearm and jerked his head. Those two walked back over to the open door and halted there. For a moment Hugh said nothing, he only gazed over towards the main house.

'She was for letting me through, Jack. I asked her to think about the things I told her that night. Things like the uselessness of a war between our two outfits.'

'She came up with the right decisions,' murmured Coleman. 'I sure felt down in the dumps when I thought she hadn't, though. You know, I've already told you twice that I've known Meredith Fortier since she was a little girl in pigtails.' Coleman paused to gently glance across the soft-lighted yard and sombrely shake his head. 'It *had* to be something else,' he muttered scarcely louder than a whisper. 'I knew it just plain *had* to be. This wasn't like her at all, Hugh.'

Hugh looked gravely around at Coleman. 'And Ed Morrow . . . ?' he inquired.

Coleman put his shoulders to the doorjamb

before he answered that, and his voice was almost gentle as he said, 'He's one of those men that won't change. That's all I can say about it, Hugh. There was a day when the things he's done weren't considered exactly wrong.' Coleman looked solemnly out into the star-washed night. 'But times have changed even though Ed hasn't.'

For a moment longer those two stood gravely over by the door lost in the tangled depths of their private thoughts and irrevocably divided by a quarter century.

Tex Rathbone walked over, eased outside between them and stood like a hunting dog with his head lifted, with his nose high as though keening the night. He turned and said, 'Riders comin',' and stepped past to re-enter the bunkhouse.

Those two words electrified every man in the Fortier bunkhouse. Even the prisoner, as Stumpy leaned over to raise his gag again, said, 'Move me away from the damned doorway. Ed'll fight.'

Stumpy obliged. He finished with the gag then roughly rolled Wes over near a tier of bunks.

Art Cowan had been rummaging a cupboard. He now went to the bunkhouse table and spilled two boxes of Winchester shells upon it. He also spilled a box of six-shooter slugs slightly apart from the longer, thinner carbine bullets. 'Load up your belts,' he said a trifle sharply. 'Once the show opens we may not have a whole lot of time.'

Hugh stepped back inside with Jack Coleman. They eased the bunkhouse door nearly closed. It was now possible to hear riders walking their horses along from the south-eastward, from the direction of Fortier Pass and the yonder foothills.

'At least,' breathed Hugh, 'they didn't hit my herd again. I reckon I ought to be thankful for that.'

'Only providin',' spoke up Tex from over by a little soiled front window, 'you're still alive tomorrow to see that herd again.'

For a while longer those oncoming riders were audible, then there was a long moment of total silence as they seemingly passed over heavy grass or something similar which muffled all sounds. When they could be heard again the riders were just beyond the yard. It was at this point that Johnny Emerson said, 'It doesn't sound like all of 'em.'

Hugh turned back from the door, stepped over where their captive was lying still as stone, bent over and yanked off the man's gag. 'Quiet now,' he warned, caught Wes by the shoulder and yanked him upright. 'They're going to wonder where you are,' he said, holding the cowboy in a hard grip. 'When they call out you answer; tell them you're in the bunkhouse.' He gave Wes a push towards the door where Coleman halted the cowboy's

170

stumbling advance with an outflung arm. Coleman whispered a warning which Wes obeyed. He stood there looking out, watching the empty yard along with the others, waiting for the first of those men to ride on into plain sight, but he made no rash move and he uttered not a sound.

Tex hissed over to Hugh: 'Watch there behind the shoeing shed. That's where they'll come into sight.'

Tex was right. Two men appeared out of the darkness riding a loose rein, sitting slumped, both of them astride bay horses. Behind these two was a large, thicker man. He was astride a horse that looked bay also, but since this animal had a light mane and tail he could not be a bay. Hugh let his breath out slowly.

The man further back said something. The two forward riders halted and looked back. For a moment the three of them conversed. Finally, one of the forward men dismounted, handed over his reins and started off around the blacksmith shop in the direction of the main house.

Coleman put forth a hand to catch Hugh's attention but he said nothing. His meaning though was amply clear. The man they couldn't quite make out over there on his chestnut horse had sent one of those cowboys on over to check Meredith's residence. Probably to find their sentry over there.

Hugh waited an agonising moment. If those

men became suspicious they would withdraw into the night. Then the boot would be on the other foot because less than a half-dozen armed men in that bunkhouse would be stationary targets for other men who had complete mobility outside.

He still clung to his wish to avoid a fight, but he was not now so entirely convinced this could be accomplished. Those waiting men on across the yard turned and faded out over there while they waited for their companion to return.

'He suspects something,' whispered Coleman. 'Otherwise he'd have ridden right on in.'

Johnny Emerson said, 'They probably got it figured out that maybe we didn't bed-down in the foothills after all; that maybe we snuck around 'em an' got up here some place.'

This seemed reasonable to Hugh. Certainly bold and fierce old Ed Morrow was not now acting as he ordinarily would have acted, especially in his own ranch-yard.

Someone made an unrealistic night-bird whistle from over at the main house. At once Marshal Coleman gripped their captive and drew him up closer to the open door. 'He hasn't found you,' Coleman breathed, 'an' he's warning the others you're not around. Call over to him.' Coleman accompanied this order with a gun-barrel poked into Wes's side hard enough to make the prisoner stifle a gasp of pain.

Hugh turned. All of them were watching the prisoner. Wes wet his lips, rolled his eyes around at those shadowy blurs which were tough-set faces, and he called out.

'Hey, is that you, Will? This is Wes. I'm over at the bunkhouse.'

For a moment there was silence. Then it wasn't the man at the main-house who called back, it was the unmistakably deep and resonant voice of Morrow answering, and he sounded outraged.

'What in the hell you doing in the bunkhouse? Told you to watch that house. Not to let no one in or out.'

Wes said, in a failing way, 'I didn't feel good, Ed.' He didn't sound good either, perhaps with sufficient reason, because Tex Rathbone, fifteen feet away on Wes's left, had that wicked-bladed big knife of his out, and where starshine hit the metal there was a cold brightness. Tex was grinning straight over at the prisoner.

For a moment the silence continued. They could see the cowboy at the main-house moving along the porch. He was a dark blur against the lighter shadows of the housefront. Suddenly he halted, bent from the waist as though staring at something in the dust beyond the porch decking, stepped over and picked something up, and Tex Rathbone groaned at his window.

'Wes's carbine,' Tex moaned. 'I kicked it out there when I knocked him over the head.'

Suddenly that shadow over there sprang around the corner of the house and flashed across a little opening heading back the way he had come.

'Cat's out of the bag now,' ripped out Hugh, and turned upon the captive. 'Call over there; tell Morrow to come over here and help you, that you're bad off.'

Wes started to obey. He had his lips parted to call out when a gunshot blew the night apart with its crimson flash and its savage thunder. Wes closed his mouth and stumbled backwards, hastily retreating deeper into the room as a bullet struck vibratingly into the outside log wall.

'Wes!' Morrow called out in his bull-bass, rolling voice. 'They got you prisoner in there?'

Tex Rathbone took long aim towards the sound of that voice, and fired. Someone across the yard let out a yelp, a startled curse, and the sound of riders frantically spurring for cover came back.

Coleman and Hugh exchanged a good long look. Coleman said resignedly, 'Well; it was a fair try. At least our intentions were to take 'em alive.' He drew his gun and flagged towards the yard with it. 'Now—let's see if we can take 'em *dead*!'

# CHAPTER SEVENTEEN

For almost a full ten minutes after Tex Rathbone fired at the sound of Ed Morrow's voice there wasn't a sound anywhere. It was so quiet the men inside the bunkhouse could easily distinguish old Stumpy's asthmatic breathing.

Wes was seated at the bunkhouse table well back from the doorway. He said in a quiet, tense tone of voice: 'They'll fire this damned building.'

Hugh, caught by that suggestion, ran a look around. Except for the one front door and the one little glass window where Tex Rathbone was keeping watch, there was no other way into or out of the bunkhouse, and no other means for seeing out either.

Coleman grunted, threw up his pistol and fired at a blurry shadow. At once two rapid six-gun shots came back. One went wild but the other one struck the door, which whipped around striking Marshal Coleman. He staggered, recovered, and laconically said, 'That's the first time I've ever been hit by proxy.'

'Who's proxy?' asked Tex, then forgot to wait for an answer as a carbine flashed redly and a bullet took out the window glass beside him. Tex dropped his head, threw up both

175

arms, and waited until cascading glass ceased falling. He afterwards looked around and said, 'By gawd, at least there's one of 'em over there full of fight.'

Wes, on the floor now underneath the bunkhouse table, had an answer for Tex. 'That's Ed Morrow himself,' he said. 'No man livin' shoots at Ed without getting one back.'

Tex looked down under the table. 'I didn't shoot at him,' he said. 'He shot at me.'

Stumpy hobbled over near Marshal Coleman and Hugh with his buffalo rifle. The bore of this weapon was large enough for a man to insert his thumb with room to spare. Stumpy couldn't stand very well, so he edged around until one shoulder, part of his head, and the barrel of that formidable gun was around the doorjamb, where it met the floor. Stumpy didn't make a sound, he simply lay there waiting.

Johnny Emerson eased over to take the opposite side of Tex's little window. He could see northward better than the others could, and when he suddenly swore, poked his carbine out and fired, none of the others had any idea where he was firing.

Four thunderous gunshots came back but Johnny was crouched down beneath the window. They struck jarringly into the outer log wall.

Hugh, able to spot one of those muzzleblasts in the darkness, fired, levered up

176

and fired again. For a long moment no return-fire came back. When it finally did, the gunman out there was a good fifty feet from where he'd been when he fired back at Johnny.

But that man had made a fatal mistake. When he spitefully fired at Hugh's muzzleblast he revealed his own position adequately for Stumpy to catch him before he'd lowered his gun to move on again.

The buffalo rifle made a sound so loud and deafening, especially within the close confines of those four log walls, that even Tex and Johnny, who were furthest away, couldn't hear a thing for five minutes afterwards.

But that tumbling, oversized slug caught the Fortier cowboy flush. It knocked him staggeringly six feet away from the edge of an outbuilding where the defenders could see him twisting in a writhing plunge. He struck the ground violently and never moved again.

Somewhere over by the main-house Ed Morrow evidently had also witnessed this terrible execution, for he bellowed for his remaining men to close in on the bunkhouse and pin down its defenders.

Hugh, placing that roaring voice, fired twice in its general direction, then desisted because as Morrow moved, he came closer to the ranch-house's front walls. Meredith would be wide awake in there someplace now. Even Marshal Coleman, with his six-gun up and tracking the sound of Morrow's voice, slowly lowered the weapon. 'Too chancy,' he said, and swung to watch the other places from which gunfire was beginning to come now in an increasing flash and roar.

Hugh, though, kept straining to catch sight of movement over at the house. He had an idea that whatever Morrow was up to over there involved Meredith, and the notion chilled him. This was no battle to involve a girl in.

The men of Fortier Valley stepped up their gunfire knocking splinters out of the log bunkhouse, driving the defenders away from the window and door. Hugh dropped down, belly-crawled up until he was opposite Stumpy where he could still see the main-house, and eventually his recklessness permitted him a glimpse of a movement. He pushed forward his carbine, snugged it back and fired. The shadow over there stopped stock-still, drew fully upright, then turned and took two big steps back off the porch disappearing around the edge of the house.

'Missed,' Hugh muttered, but only Stumpy heard him and Stumpy was tracking a foe of his own down the sight of that bull-throated cannon of his and paid Hugh no heed.

The attacker-fire began to atrophy as men fired themselves out and had to pause for reloading. This gave Tex, Johnny Emerson and Marshal Coleman the chance they'd been waiting for. Each of them stepped back to their vantage points and raked the yonder outbuildings with a furious volley.

For another five minutes it was the defending men who controlled this savage battle, but when they also began to run out of shells, the attackers, freshly reloaded and impatient for their licks, took over again. This see-sawing back and forth continued for nearly half an hour and during it, when he was able to do so, Hugh kept a worried vigil towards Meredith's house. He was almost certain that Morrow had got around the back somewhere, had got inside, and by now had Meredith as his hostage.

A bullet came out of nowhere, struck Stumpy's exposed barrel knocking the gun violently upwards. The heavy oaken stock crashed with considerable force against its owner's jaw and Stumpy's head jerked, his hat flew half across the room, and he afterwards fell across his gun, knocked senseless.

Hugh dropped flat, rolled over, caught Stumpy's uninjured leg and dragged him out of harm's way. He and Johnny rolled the *cosinero* over expecting to see blood and torn flesh, saw only the growing welt alongside Stumpy's jaw, and with looks of enormous relief pushed him closer to the wall where he wouldn't be hit by bullets or trampled underfoot.

The diminished return-fire while Johnny and Hugh and Stumpy were out of the immediate fight seemed to encourage

Morrow's men. One of them even called over a derisive insult to the men in the bunkhouse. They all stepped up their gunfire again and Marshal Coleman, ducking from a slug which hit the door with exceptional force, flattened his shoulders against the wall and made a wry face at Hugh.

'Warm night out,' he called over. Even Johnny Emerson grinned at Coleman's coolness. It was the first look Johnny had shown any of them, other than expressions of violent disapproval, since they'd buried Milt Stillwell.

But Johnny's smile got wiped off the moment he stood up and turned towards the little wrecked window. He twisted further. He dropped down and peered under the table where their captive was. He straightened up and said: 'Where the hell is Tex?'

Rathbone was no longer in the bunkhouse with them!

For a moment they stood gazing blankly at the window. It did not seem possible for anyone to have left the bunkhouse and yet obviously Tex had.

From his place of safety Wes called into a brief lull in the firing to say he'd seen Rathbone leave, had seen him spring out the window while the others had been concerned over Stumpy.

'He'll never make it,' breathed Emerson. But Wes thought differently and said so.

'He went out that window slick as a cat. I heard him hit down outside and run around the building northward. I wouldn't bet he won't make it. That feller's fast as greased lightning.'

Hugh and Coleman resumed their vigil by the door. Johnny stepped over to the window again. Outside darkness hid much of the yonder yard, but where there were no shadowing buildings visibility was still good even though the moon was rapidly dropping away now.

Hugh sighted movement, dry-fired his carbine at it. The gun was empty. He leaned it aside and drew his .45. By that time whoever that was over there flitting from building to building, was gone.

That same high-pitched taunting voice called out derisively again. It named no names but it told the men in the bunkhouse they didn't have a chance. Johnny swore aloud at whomever that was and fired blindly towards the sound of the voice. He at once harvested a ragged fusillade which drove him down below the sill.

Hugh and Coleman opened up again, sighting at muzzleblasts. The outside gunmen swung to return this fire which permitted Emerson to straighten up and get off several rounds of his own. Art Cowan joined him in this furious firing.

Emboldened by the diminished gunfire

coming from their bunkhouse, the men of Fortier Valley moved in still closer, some flattening alongside buildings, some stepping forth to shoot, then springing back again. Their accuracy improved too. Bullets came through the doorway into the room. Several ricocheted, causing frantic Wes to roll up into a ball under his table, making of himself as small a target as possible.

Once, as he reloaded, Hugh said to Marshal Coleman, 'That damned Texan,' in strong condemnation. But Coleman, searching for a yonder target, had an answer to that which he gave without looking around.

'I don't think so, Hugh. That feller's already proved himself mighty slippery and mighty handy according to my standards. He scouted the way and brought us here without a hitch. I wouldn't underestimate him now. As a matter of fact I've been thinkin' I'd a lot rather be in here with him on my side, than out there in the dark with him slippin' around with that eight-inch clasp-knife of his, looking for a back to stick it into.'

Suddenly a rifle opened up from over at the main-house. The battlers, unexpecting this on both sides, held off for as long as it took them to peer around and see who this gunman might be and which direction he was firing in. After three fast shots that gun was briefly silent, then it flashed a fourth time. That time a man yelped over by the blacksmith shop and they all distinctly heard a carbine rake over wooden siding as that man turned and hastily legged it away from where he'd been.

Now the silence returned, only it was more lethal now, more deadly. Coleman stepped out, stared, jumped back and held his breath. No bullet came. He looked across the doorway to Hugh and said, 'It must be your Texan. He got to the house.'

Hugh was perplexed and worried. 'Morrow's over there, probably inside. He'll back-shoot Tex.'

They both got a surprise when Johnny Emerson called softly, saying in puzzlement: 'What the hell's goin' on out there? I just saw Tex jump inside the shoein' shed.'

'It couldn't have been Tex,' stated Coleman. 'He's the one firin' from the house.'

Hugh broke in saying, 'Wait a minute, you two. Could that be *Meredith* at the house?'

'How?' said Coleman bluntly. 'You just said yourself you saw Morrow headin' for the house.'

Hugh shook his head. He had to admit it didn't make any sense. Meredith was a girl— she couldn't possibly cope with Ed Morrow with guns.

Someone northward threw a slug towards the main-house. At once that mysterious carbine answered back driving a slug close enough to the yonder man to make him duck for cover. 'Hey,' he roared in an aggrieved, indignant tone. 'What the hell you think you're doing over there? Ed, you're shootin' at your own men.'

Hugh and Marshal Coleman and Johnny Emerson got the answer to their little mystery when Meredith Fortier's unmistakable voice answered that cowboy.

'This isn't Ed. This is Meredith Fortier. I pay your wages and I give the orders. You put down your guns and come over here to the main-house.'

There wasn't a sound anywhere. This unique hush built up and drew out to its absolute maximum. Within the bunkhouse Stumpy moaned and awkwardly moved, reminding the others that he was still in this battle. Outside, a man's slow, dragging voice spoke up sounding sullen, sounding uncertain.

'Miss Meredith, where's Ed? He give us orders to wipe out them trespassers in there. He said . . .'

'I told you,' came back Meredith's spirited, sharp voice. 'I give the orders in Fortier Valley. Now you put down those guns and come over here!'

'But ma'am,' whined another man, this one over near the shoeing shed. 'Where's Ed?'

'Ed,' came back the lovely girl's angry retort, 'is shot through the body and lying in here on my parlour floor. And in case he didn't tell you boys, I'll tell you something that he told me: one of the men in the bunkhouse you're trying to kill is U.S. Marshal Jack Coleman from Denver. Those are not all Mister Benedict's riders in there. *Now put down those guns and come over here!'*

Hugh stepped away from the door, looked at Johnny, looked at Coleman, dropped his head and began to mechanically reload his six-gun. When he'd completed this he dropped the weapon into its hip-holster, stepped back to the door and despite Jack Coleman's hissed warning, walked on out of the riddled little log building. Nothing happened. None of the attacking cowboys were anywhere in sight, but if they saw him now, they did not shoot.

Directly across the yard a man was suddenly and very roughly propelled out into the dusty yard. This was one of the Fortier Ranch men, but his holster was empty and as he caught himself and halted out there, fully exposed, he twisted to stare back over his shoulder. The drawl of Tex Rathbone spoke forward to this man loud enough for all to hear.

'Do like the lady says, cowboy. Walk on over to the house.'

The cowboy obediently began to walk, but he did it stiffly and unnaturally, as though expecting a bullet in the back every step of the way.

Hugh stepped down and also started forward. Other men appeared, also striding forward. Finally Johnny and Marshal Coleman, supporting Stumpy, came out too.

The battle was over.

## CHAPTER EIGHTEEN

Meredith was there in her doorway with a carbine balanced across in front of her, held by both hands. She saw Hugh and Marshal Coleman, Johnny Emerson and Stumpy Crawford. She also gazed out at her own men, her face both angry and flushed.

'No guns,' she said. 'Leave them outside and step in here.'

Her ranch-hands, being careful to rigidly avoid looking over at their dishevelled enemies, shed a pistol here and there and trooped forward. Meredith stepped out onto the porch to allow them to pass. 'Light a lamp in there,' she ordered, then turned as Marshal Coleman stepped up, still wearing his sidearm. 'I said no guns, Marshal.'

Coleman gazed down into her troubled face. 'Sorry, Meredith; regulations say no U.S. Marshal goes unarmed in the performance of his duty.' Coleman hesitated, then reached for her Winchester. For just a second she did not relinquish it. Both their hands held that weapon. Then she let go and slumped against the bullet-marked front wall. Coleman smiled at her. He said in a voice almost too low for the others to hear: 'I knew it was in you to see what was right and decent, honey. I only prayed you'd do it before it was too late.'

Coleman passed on inside. Johnny Emerson, half-supporting Stumpy Crawford, crowded on past too. The last one in was Hugh. He paused to gaze a moment into Meredith Fortier's drawn, pale countenance, then without a word he too passed into the house.

She closed the door. For a while all those men stood stiffly and awkwardly eyeing one another. Someone had lifted Ed Morrow, had made him comfortable upon a large leather sofa. He looked grey and lifeless as Hugh stepped up beside Coleman and gazed downwards. Morrow was rational and perfectly conscious of everything around him. He stared dryly up at Hugh for a long time, then shifted his gaze to Marshal Coleman.

'She'd wanted to let 'em through,' he said past stiffening lips. 'Marshal, she was goin' to compromise.'

'She should have, Ed,' said Coleman, pulling up a chair and dropping down athwart it.

Morrow weakly rolled his massive, bearded face from side to side. 'No, Jack, no. Her paw told me—never let her give an inch. He told me—never let her show weakness. Keep her—safe. Jules told me on his deathbed—do her thinkin' for her, Ed, she's only a female.'

Coleman looked around where the others

were gathered on opposite sides of the room. He saw Meredith leaning whitely with her back to the closed front door. He looked up at Hugh beside him, then down again. He gently shook his head at Morrow.

'Did he tell you to kill like this, Ed?'

'Who—got killed, Jack?'

'That stampede you started pulverised a young cowboy, Ed. Ground him into a bloody froth.'

Morrow ran a sluggish tongue over his lips, flicked a dimming glance upwards at Hugh, and for a moment a dark shadow of his former black stubbornness showed. Then he said to Coleman, 'I kept my word to—Jules. That's all. I did my best—to keep my word.'

Coleman nodded without speaking. He bent far over, caught hold of a folded afghan, shook it out and with a surprising degree of tenderness, drew the thing up over Ed Morrow covering him from boots to shoulders with it.

'A man always tries to keep his word,' he said gently. 'I know how it is, Ed. Only, this is a dead man's range, and the dead have no right to keep a hold on the living. Times change, Ed, which the dead don't know.'

'I—kept—my word,' sighed big Ed Morrow, and let out a long, soft breath.

Coleman said, 'Amen.' He looked at Hugh. 'He's dead. On every man's gravestone should be carved some reference to his outstanding virtue. On Ed Morrow's I reckon we can put

188

that he kept his word.'

Tex Rathbone and Art Cowan, standing side by side facing across towards the sullen-looking men of Fortier Valley, were quietly speaking in a low tone. Stumpy, nearer Ed Morrow's couch and seated, shot them both a dark look and shook his head. Neither Tex nor Art knew Morrow had died but Stumpy's dour look and little head-shake warned them, so they looked across towards the couch and became silent.

The room was utterly still except for the breathing of men, as Marshal Coleman pushed up off his chair, bent, lifted the knitted afghan and placed it tenderly over the dead man's face. He afterwards turned and ran a slow, slow look around at the others. He was the only armed man in that room, but this wasn't the only reason they watched him. Jack Coleman was a man who commanded attention even without his badge.

'Morrow is dead,' he pronounced. 'I wish I could let it end there, but I can't. He was responsible for what's happened here the last two days, you Fortier riders did what he told you to do. That will probably count with the court, but a cowboy got trampled to death in the stampede yesterday, and that's murder in the eyes of the law. I reckon I might manage to get the charges of attempted murder and attackin' a peace officer dropped for what's happened here tonight. But you Fortier riders are under arrest. You'll have to go down to Denver with me an' be tried.' Coleman looked over at Meredith. 'I'm sorry,' he concluded. 'If ever there was a senseless battle this was it. I'm sorry, boys.'

Meredith paced quietly over to stand briefly gazing down at her dead rangeboss, then she ran out of the room. The men stood awkwardly silent. Even Johnny Emerson and old Stumpy Crawford didn't look fierce any more. Hugh and Cowan and Tex Rathbone looked at their boots. The Fortier Ranch riders, shy two of their numbers including that man Stumpy had downed with his buffalo gun as well as Ed Morrow, looked dispirited, looked demoralised and bewildered now that they were leaderless.

Coleman looked at Tex saying, 'Fetch Wes from the bunkhouse, will you?'

Rathbone turned wordlessly towards the door, passed on out and they all distinctly heard his footfalls crunching through the ranch-yard dust.

Coleman removed his hat, dragged a soiled sleeve across his forehead and dropped the hat back on again. He gazed over at Hugh. 'You can prefer charges,' he said. 'There'll be the recovery for the cattle lost in the stampede, for the horses, for Stumpy's injury.'

Stumpy looked up indignantly at Marshal Coleman. 'What injury?' he said. 'A horse can fall with a man any time, stampede or no stampede. I ain't pressin' no charges against no one.'

Hugh, considering his crestfallen enemies, shook his head. He ran a glance over to the doorway where Meredith had disappeared, and found that she'd returned, at least as far as that doorway, and was standing there now with one hand upon the wall, watching all this and listening. She met his glance head-on.

Hugh said, 'You have your duty, Jack, but I've got no stomach for any more of this. It's ended. We all know what happened; what made Morrow do what he did. All I want to do now is get back to my wagon, break camp and head on out of here. If I lose some cattle on the Fort Collins trace, why I reckon I'll just have to lose them.'

Meredith said quietly, 'No. You bring your herd up through Fortier Valley. I told Ed that's what I wanted the last time he and I spoke about it. I told him I didn't want any more fighting.'

Hugh gazed across the room at her without speaking. He felt drained dry, incapable of dredging up any emotion, embittered. 'Three dead men,' he murmured to her. 'I can't just step over their bodies and forget them, Meredith.'

She looked straight at him, her beautiful face wan and grey, her smoke-coloured eyes dry looking. 'Brooding never helps, and no tribulation is worth anything, Hugh, unless people learn from it. I've learned. I'd learned even before anyone was hurt. But my mistake was in not facing Ed with a gun. That way I could have stopped him. I tried to with words—and wound up a prisoner in my own house, on my own ranch.' She gently shook her head at him. 'The dead are dead and the living must go on living. You bring your herd up through Fortier Valley.'

Marshal Coleman, looking from one of them to the other, cleared his throat, looked at Art Cowan, at Johnny Emerson, and was about to speak when Tex entered the house with Wes, whose hands were no longer tied. Coleman jerked his head sideways at Wes. 'Over with your friends,' he said, and paused to reframe what he'd earlier intended to say. 'Hugh, can you loan me Tex to help take these men to town?'

Hugh broke off staring across at Meredith. 'Sure, Jack. Take Art and Johnny too, if you like. We won't be doing anything in camp today.'

'No,' said Coleman, keeping his steady gaze upon Hugh. 'Just Tex will be enough. Besides, you'll need Cowan and Emerson, and Stumpy too. Three thousand head of cattle is quite a bunch to drive up a pass they haven't been up before, an' for a few days anyway, Meredith won't have any cowboys to loan you for that purpose.'

Coleman's gaze at Hugh warmed a little,

turned fatherly and understanding. He and the younger man, each with his own thoughts, stood like that for a long moment before the lawman spoke again.

'Up through Fortier Valley, Hugh, just like you planned. On to the goldfields with your herd—then back again to Fortier Valley. It'll still be a tough drive. You'll have a couple of weeks for sweatin' and thinkin'. Those are the two best cures I know of for melancholy. Sweatin' and thinkin'.' Coleman nodded over at Tex. 'Reckon you and I better get started for town. It's a long ride an' the sun'll be up soon.' He looked at the prisoners. 'Outside, boys,' he said.

The cowboys shuffled over where Tex was holding back the door. Cowan and Emerson and Stumpy looked up as those men went by. Coleman saw this and said, 'Maybe you three wouldn't mind givin' us a hand saddlin' up.'

Cowan and Johnny nodded but Stumpy sat there in his chair. 'My leg's botherin' me a little,' he said to the lawman. 'And someone cracked m'jaw too. I'll just wait here until . . .'

'Stumpy,' interrupted Cowan in a pained voice. 'Use your head just for once, will you?' Cowan stood over there big and thick and scowling at the *cosinero*.

Stumpy was puzzled. He didn't arise and Cowan finally paced on over, bent down, whispered, then yanked the smaller and older man up out of his chair by the shoulder.

Stumpy didn't resist. He instead shot a look from Hugh to Meredith and said, 'Oh, sure, Art, sure. I didn't understand. Sure-'nough. I'm a feller as knows where he's not wanted. You don't have to—hey!—quit tuggin' on this shirt; it's the only un-torn one I got left. Let go, consarn it, I can walk.'

Cowan didn't let go. He escorted Stumpy all the way to the door and gave him a little propelling shove on through. Then Cowan jerked his head at Johnny Emerson and closed the door behind them all, leaving only Meredith and Hugh in the parlour, except for that unnaturally flat outline under the knitted afghan.

Meredith said, 'I'll send to town for more men.'

Hugh walked over to that huge old smoke-blackened fireplace, put his back to it and said, 'Who'll you send?'

Meredith looked momentarily confused. 'Yes, I forgot,' she murmured. 'Well, I'll go myself.'

He shook his head at her. 'I'll do it. You'll need those riders in the valley before my cattle get here. One of your men told me you'd been gathering. You should have riders up here to keep the herds separate before my cattle get to the top of the pass.'

'Hugh, you'll bring them through?'

He nodded.

She left the doorway to walk up within five

feet of him and halt, her hands clasped across her stomach. 'I want you to know that I tried very hard to stop it; that I gave orders you were to be allowed through.'

'I know, Meredith.'

'Don't hate Ed, Hugh. What he did he thought he had to do.'

'I understand. I'll help you bury him before I go on.'

Her knuckles were white with straining, her large grey eyes darkened towards him. 'Promise me you'll come back. Promise me . . .'

He stepped forward. 'I'll come back. I'd have come back some day regardless of how I feel now, Meredith. What I told you was the truth.'

She looked straight up at him. 'Tell me again,' she whispered.

He didn't tell her, not right then, he *showed* her. He put out his hands to sway her to him. She placed her palms upon his chest and stood up to her full height to meet his lips. It was a tender, gentle kiss and she afterwards dropped back down.

'Do you know why I fought you so hard, Hugh? Because from that first night, I was afraid of you. No, that's not exactly right. I was afraid of myself. I was afraid of what I'd let you do to me.'

He brushed aside a heavy lock of her blue-black hair and said, 'Once, right here in this room, I almost told you I loved you, Meredith.

The only reason I didn't tell you was because I was too angry to say it.'

'Then you will come back?'

'As soon as I've sold the cattle. As soon as I have enough money to . . .'

'The money doesn't mean anything, Hugh. I have plenty of that for both of us.'

He smiled at her. 'Keep yours,' he said. 'We'll use that to educate our kids with. Mine, we'll use for making Fortier Ranch the biggest, best, most hospitable cow outfit in all Colorado Territory.'

She leaned against him, buried her face against his chest and was still holding him like that when Art Cowan apologetically coughed out on the porch. 'Horses are ready, Hugh,' Art called. 'Any time you are.'

31.7.